I'm Being Stalked by a Moonshadow

DOUG MACLEOD

I'm Being Stalked by a Moonshadow

Front Street
Asheville, North Carolina

First published by Penguin Group (Australia), 2006

Printed in China
Designed by Helen Robinson
First U.S. edition, 2007

Library of Congress Cataloging-in-Publication Data

MacLeod, Doug.
I'm being stalked by a moonshadow / Doug MacLeod.
p. cm.
Summary: As his odd parents fight the regional environmental health officer about their dung-covered house and his melodramatic younger brother demands attention, fourteen-year-old Australian Seth Parrot simply seeks the muscular woman of his dreams.
ISBN 978-1-59078-501-0 (hardcover : alk. paper)
[1. Family life—Australia—Fiction.
2. Eccentrics and eccentricities—Fiction.
3. Dating (Social customs)—Fiction. 4. Schools—Fiction.
5. Australia—Fiction. 6. Humorous stories.]
I. Title. II. Title: I am being stalked by a moonshadow.
PZ7.M224945Iaam 2007
[Fic]—dc22 2006101608

Front Street
An Imprint of Boyds Mills Press, Inc.
815 Church Street
Honesdale, Pennsylvania 18431

I'm Being Stalked by a Moonshadow

A WARNING TO AMERICANS

In America, you don't have lamingtons, you have Twinkies, which are kind of the same, and if a shifting spanner fell in your lap, you'd probably call it a "wrench." By the same token, the narrator of this book wants to go abseiling, not "rappelling." An Aussie ends up in hospital if he breaks his wrists, not "in *the* hospital," like an American. Australian kids wear jumpers, play in cubby houses, and sometimes watch Pingu. (He's a Claymation penguin who actually comes from Switzerland, but for some reason he caught on Down Under.) And if someone from Australia were to call you a "dag," you shouldn't be offended ... but it'd be good to look it up.

FACT ONE

A giraffe's tongue is fifty-five centimeters long

When Mum and Dad decided to build their dream home, they bought a beautiful block of land in a suburb called Kinglet at the foot of the mountains. For a year we lived in a luxury caravan parked on the corner of the block at 17 Jacana Avenue. I helped my parents make mud bricks—huge blocks of congealed mud and straw.

Mum and Dad were at their happiest when they were filthy dirty. There were mud fights, and I'd join in, while my little brother, Jack, watched from the caravan annex, painting his fingernails and hoping he was adopted.

"You're disgusting!" Jack would cry.

"Rude gestures!" Dad would say.

"Rude gestures to *you*!"

The bellbirds would ping away, unconcerned.

When they were built, the walls of the dream home looked rough and ratty. I was disappointed. The mud bricks didn't have nice smooth surfaces, like normal bricks. But my parents weren't finished yet. What came next, and what marked the beginning of our problems, was *the rendering*.

Mum and Dad collected manure in big bins from a

nearby dairy. Then they happily sloshed the cow manure on the walls. Dad explained that people in the Middle East did this for insulation and appearance. This might have been a good idea in the deserts of Oman. But here, in the suburbs—even the outer, *outer* suburbs where hippies still lived—it struck me as a bit odd. The bellbirds certainly thought so. They stopped pinging when the walls started ponging.

But I ended up helping with the rendering. After all, it was only herbivore poo. It wasn't something truly horrible, like uranium or seafood extender. It was grass that had passed through the digestive tract of a cow. Jack kept telling us how revolting we were, and continued moisturizing under the annex.

My mother and father were slightly "alternative." They drove a Toyota with stickers on the back telling the government to stop doing things. They had long hair that they wore in ponytails, even though Jack begged them to get haircuts. Girls often fancied my father. Fortunately, Dad only fancied Mum.

Dad was an I.T. architect, though he didn't like it much. His hobby was collecting interesting facts. Thanks to Dad, I knew how long a giraffe's tongue was.

Mum worked as a professional organizer. She'd been on television once when she organized a rally to protect a colony of endangered seabirds called "brown boobies." I suspect the reason Mum got on TV was that the presenter liked saying "brown boobies." Mum ran The

Shared Learning Center, or SLC, in Kinglet. It was a place where people went to learn skills such as pottery, leadlighting, cat psychology or how to make goat's cheese (not recommended). The SLC was a real rabbit warren, as though a bunch of cubby houses had decided to get together and become one big building. It smelled of damp hessian and raw wool. It was a much better place than regular school.

Girls might have fancied Dad, but they *adored* Jack. At the age of thirteen, Jack had movie-star looks. His hair was straight and dark blond and he could gel it into incredible shapes. He had a little upturned nose and brown button eyes, as far apart as it's possible for eyes to be and still look cute rather than alien.

My face was pointy, with close-set eyes that were such a pale shade of blue they often didn't show in photos. My hair started out blond but decided to go red when I turned nine. *Very* red. And it refused to obey gravity. When I turned fourteen I had a growth spurt. Overnight, I became 180 centimeters tall—186 if you included my hair. Jack said I was starting to look like Nicole Kidman. He could be a cruel brother sometimes.

Jack also called me a pervert. This was because I liked women with big muscles. When they broadcast the Ms. Olympia bodybuilding contest on TV, I fell in love with the bronze medalist. Her name was Opal Honey, she had massive shoulders, and I wanted to marry her. I was eight at the time. Dad said my preference for muscly girls had to do with *yin* and *yang*.

•

"The yin is feminine and the yang is masculine," said Dad, strumming his guitar one night. Dad wore a necklace with a yin/yang charm on it. This is a black and white symbol from Chinese philosophy, the symbol of balance.

"I think I like girls who are yin with a tiny bit of yang," I said.

"That's all right. It probably means you're yang with a little bit of yin."

Which bit of me was yin? My hair? My nose? My vertebral aponeurosis muscle?

"No one is pure yin or pure yang," Dad said. "Everyone is a mixture of the two. And if you put together all the yin and all the yang of everyone in the world, they'd balance perfectly."

Mum entered, brushing her long black hair streaked with silver. It looked better when it wasn't tied back. The muscles in her upper arm moved as she dragged the brush through her hair. Mum probably had a pinch of yang in her arms.

"What on earth are you talking about?"

Dad decided to keep our conversation secret. "Seth and I were discussing the mating ritual of the giant panda. Did you realize, Zilla, the female panda walks around backward in order to attract a mate?"

"How interesting," said Mum.

"She also pees."

"Would you find me more attractive if I did that?"

"No. But a male panda might, so don't do it. You could

get approaches from huge Chinese bears stinking of bamboo shoots."

"I might enjoy that," said Mum.

"You're both idiots," I said.

"Rude gestures!" said Dad.

"Rude gestures to *you*!"

"And now we're going to have a singalong," Dad said. "Seth, do you have a request?"

"I request not to be part of this singalong."

Dad started strumming an old hippy song called "Moonshadow" by Cat Stevens. This was one of my parents' favorites. Mum sang along. Soon she and Dad were laughing together. I knew that when the song was finished they'd run off to the master bedroom, and since we were still in the luxury caravan, that was only eighteen centimeters away. They had a very healthy physical relationship.

Dad, Mum, Jack and I lived a fairly happy life. Our trials didn't begin until we started rendering the house and my father made a mortal enemy.

It was the middle of summer, the start of a new millennium, and we were about to move into the dream home. While Dad and Mum and I were rendering, we received a visit from a representative of the local council. He handed over a business card. It said his name was Jeff Raven, the senior environmental health officer for the district of Currawong. He was a humorless bald man with a clipboard. Even though it was a hot day, the top button of his spotless white shirt was done up and his tie firmly knotted.

"Can we help you?" asked Mum.

"There have been complaints," said Mr. Raven.

"What about?" asked Dad.

"You're putting dung on your walls. The smell is most offensive."

"We're rendering." Dad explained all about insulation and the Middle East.

"We aren't in the Middle East," said Mr. Raven. "We're in a residential street."

"It's our house," said Dad. "Surely we can do what we want."

"This is a serious matter. Please stop what you're doing."

Dad tossed his trowel into the nearest bin of muck. He did it carelessly and a fleck splashed onto Mr. Raven's gray creased pants.

"Sorry," said Mum.

"I think Mr. Parrot should apologize," said Mr. Raven, "since he's the one who flicked dung at me."

"It wasn't deliberate," said Dad.

"I still think you should apologize."

But Dad didn't apologize.

"Please tell us what exactly the issue is," said Mum.

"The smell. People don't like it."

Mum reassured Mr. Raven. "After it dries it won't smell."

"I'll have to visit again when your walls are dry and smell them to make sure."

Mr. Raven looked at me. I was covered in muck. He

shook his head in disgust, then straightened his tie unnecessarily and strode off.

"What an officious man!" said Dad.

"You shouldn't have flicked poo at him," said Mum.

"It was an accident."

"Are you sure?"

"It was only a tiny speck, Zilla." Dad went back to work. "I wonder who reported us? Perhaps it was Mr. Robbins?"

Our silver-haired neighbor was quietly tending to his flowers in his back garden.

"Mr. Robbins is far too nice to report us," said Mum, waving her trowel at him.

Mr. Robbins smiled and waved back.

At the Shared Learning Center, Zoran the gardener shook his head in dismay when I told him what my parents had done to the house. In Serbia he had been an accountant. But he couldn't find any accountancy work in Australia. Zoran disliked gardening and refused to learn the names of any of the flowers. He just called them Serbian swear words.

"Why they do this, Set? Don't they like house?" said Zoran.

"It's supposed to be ecological," I said.

"You help your parents to put this cacka on wall?"

"How did you guess?"

"You stink like gypsy donkey."

"It's not me, it's your fertilizer."

Zoran sniffed his bag of fertilizer. "Maybe you right. But you still dirty boy. In Serbia they put boys like you in prison. You lucky to live in free country like Australia. In Serbia you can't do nothing. You need permit to eat sandwich in park."

Zoran emptied his bag of fertilizer straight onto the flowers.

I screwed up my nose. "Aren't you supposed to put that *around* them?"

"I hate these flowers," said Zoran.

I asked Zoran why he was so miserable all the time. Was he lonely? Did he have a serious girlfriend?

"I am married since I was eighteen. In Serbia many people marry young."

"Is your wife in Australia?" I asked.

"It is very sad story." Zoran gave me a look of deep despair. "Yes, she is."

Mum was right. The cow manure smell did go away and the walls looked good—smooth and light brown with the occasional sprig of dried clover. We moved into the dream home and sold the luxury caravan.

Mum was drinking a glass of wheatgrass juice when Mr. Raven called to smell our walls. When she offered him some wheatgrass juice he said he'd prefer plain water. Mum gave him water in a black cup.

"Could I please have it in a clear glass?" asked Mr. Raven.

Mum politely gave Mr. Raven water in a clear glass.

He held it up to the light. "This glass has greasy fingerprints on it."

Dad snapped. He took the glass from Mr. Raven and examined it closely.

"My God, you're right! Zilla, destroy this glass immediately. It has human fingerprints. It's disgusting."

"Eric, stop it!"

"And there are some fingerprints on the fridge. We'll have to destroy that as well." Dad was in full flight. I could see Mum getting mad. "My God, there are fingerprints absolutely everywhere! We'll just have to burn everything, starting with the children."

"Eric!" Mum growled.

Eventually, Mr. Raven had to admit that the walls were indeed odorless. Dad suggested that Mr. Raven should concentrate on more serious matters. This annoyed Mr. Raven, who immediately found fault with the toilet door.

"It opens inward, not outward," said Mr. Raven. "It doesn't conform to regulations. I'll have to send a building inspector."

"There's no need," said Mum. "We'll fix the problem. Thank you for pointing it out to us."

"Good day to you," said Mr. Raven, turning away.

"Chromedome," muttered Dad under his breath.

Mr. Raven stopped in his tracks. "Excuse me, did you just call me chromedome?"

"Certainly not," said Dad.

The senior environmental health officer for the district of Currawong left.

"Eric, sometimes you can be a dingbat," said Mum.

Dad was a good carpenter and he fixed the toilet door in no time, though he was angry about being made to do it. He preferred a door that opened inward and not outward. I helped because I was a devoted son and also Dad paid me. Jack watched and complained when some sawdust stuck to the green gloss he was applying to his toenails.

The next day we saw Mr. Raven walking up our front path.

"Don't you dare say anything silly to Mr. Raven," Mum warned Dad as she went to answer the door. "If you do, I'll jump on your guitar."

Mr. Raven spent half an hour inspecting our kitchen. He said he had concerns about it.

"I can fetch you a microscope," Dad offered.

"That won't be necessary," Mr. Raven replied.

"Would you like a drink of water?" Dad asked. "We have a glass in the sterilizer."

"I'm fine."

When Mr. Raven had his back turned, Mum pretended to jump on Dad's guitar, to make Dad behave. Mr. Raven continued his job in stony silence.

"Can I offer you something to eat, Mr. Raven?" suggested Mum. "Perhaps some carrot cake?"

"No, thank you."

"It's very good for constipation," said Dad.

Mum did more guitar-jumping mimes at Dad. Mr. Raven caught Mum in the middle of her mime act. She pretended she was trying to stomp on a bug.

"This kitchen is not a healthy food preparation area," Mr. Raven said, handing us a list of things to fix. "Please attend to these matters as soon as possible."

Then he left.

"This means war," said Dad.

FACT TWO

An e-mail bomb is just a huge bunch of e-mails

Our local paper is famous for its misprints. There was an article in it about how someone had sent an e-mail bomb to Mr. Jeff Raven (39), the senior environmental health pofficer for the district of Currabong. Mr. Raven was quoted as saying that it was the act of a cyber-terrorist, who would be found and punished. The e-mail bomb had been sent by someone calling himself William Shatner.

"It was you, wasn't it?" said Mum.

Dad looked the picture of innocence, the way Jack does when he's done something bad, which is often.

"Zilla, I'm sure I don't know what you're talking about." Dad continued to read the paper.

Mum wasn't buying it. "You sent that e-mail bomb to get back at Jeff Raven. Vengeance is an ugly trait."

"So is being a nasty little bald man who made me spend a fortune on the kitchen. And it wasn't a very harmful bomb. I'm quite nice to computers."

"I wish you were nicer to people."

Jack couldn't wait to tell his friends about Dad sending the e-mail bomb. Dad told him to keep it secret. I.T. architects aren't supposed to do things like that. He might lose his job if his boss found out.

If he were going to keep quiet, Jack wanted something in return.

"Dad, can I get a stud in my ear?" he asked.

"If you like," said Dad.

"What about one in my nose?"

"You don't need one in your nose," Mum said. "You're already handsome enough."

This was true. People found it hard to believe that Jack and I were brothers. I was used to the disappointed looks from girls that Jack brought home, when they saw that his older brother was nowhere near as gorgeous as they'd expected.

"What about my tongue?" asked Jack. "Can I get a stud in my tongue?"

"Definitely not your tongue," said Mum.

We had a roast chicken for dinner, and Jack found the wishbone. He and I curled our little fingers around it, made a wish, then broke the bone. My wish was for a serious girlfriend who looked like Opal Honey. But Jack got the bigger part. He told us that he'd wished for world peace. I knew he hadn't because if you say your wish out loud it doesn't come true. He'd probably wished for a mobile phone.

That night I did sixty push-ups in my bedroom. The picture of Opal Honey on my wall was an inspiration. I was determined to have a girlfriend like her one day. But I'd have to work hard. I was not only quite lean, I was also hopeless with girls. Whenever I spoke with them I panicked and started telling them stuff like how long a giraffe's tongue is. Jack never had any trouble. He always knew what to say, and girls loved it when he called them "precious." I was just starting on my sit-ups when I heard a group of feral kids outside chanting, "Poo house poo house poo house!" They'd been doing this since the rendering. "Shut up, you little maggots!" Dad yelled, but it didn't work.

A new drama teacher started work at the SLC. His name was Will Stretton. He was short and bearded. Mum was keen for Jack and me to sign up for his course. It seemed a good idea. Jack wanted to be an actor. I wanted to meet muscular girls. Surely there'd be at least one in the class.

Will made everyone in the class wear tights, even chubby Tyrone the baker, who was twenty. Besides Tyrone, Jack and me, there were eight other people in the class. Two were identical twins called Casper and Jasper. They were always biting each other and scrapping, like a pair of Tasmanian devils. There was a dark girl called Poppy, who wrote poetry and was far too thin. There was a highly superstitious girl called Nangret. Once she saw two teaspoons crossed on a saucer and said this was a bad omen. Three days later, there was a mudslide in Guatemala. "Told you," said Nangret. There was a boy called Lukas who seemed to have limited language skills.

I think his parents might have been using the SLC as a child-minding center. Lukas also did ikebana and fish care.

There was a girl called India, who was blonde and varnished and fragrant. She was Jack's type. It wouldn't be long before Jack would start calling India "precious," and they'd exchange cute little kisses. Girls never said no to Jack.

There were no muscular girls like Opal Honey in the class. Not one of the girls looked like she might enjoy a healthy arm wrestle before breakfast. According to Zoran, there were plenty of girls like this in Serbia. I was considering emigrating there.

We did acting exercises, like pretending to be an animal. Everyone chose lively animals like monkeys and gazelles, and pranced about. Nangret chose a white cat because they're lucky, although she snagged her tights badly when she tried to chase an imaginary mouse. I thought I'd be a jaguar because they have powerful bodies. But seeing everyone running around like idiots made me decide to choose an owl instead. I had a little doze in the corner because owls are nocturnal. In another game we had to say "Wahhh!" in a loud and convincing way. Will Stretton said all actors did this, though I couldn't picture Nicole Kidman wandering round Hollywood saying, "Wahhh!"

Another thing we did was read plays. There was one called *Medea*, about a Greek woman who finds herself at a loose end one afternoon and chops up her children. This was two thousand years ago, before social workers. I thought it was a great play and decided that writing plays might be something I could do to make money. I didn't know what I wanted to do for a living, only that I wanted to make money.

As I read Greek plays in my bedroom that summer, the feral kids outside kept chanting, "Poo house!" over and over. I could understand why Medea went mad with the hatchet. One night Dad and I decided to reason with the kids, since yelling had failed.

"This is not a poo house," Dad told the small group of kids on their bikes. The eldest would have been ten. "This is a poo-*rendered* house."

The kids burst out laughing, as if living in a poo-rendered house was even worse than living in one constructed entirely from poo. A kid threw a lump of dirt at my father and it hit him in the chest. Dad let out a grunt of surprise. Cackling, the kids rode off into the dusk.

"Are you all right, Dad?"

"I'm fine, Seth."

Dad put his arm around my shoulders as we walked back into the house.

It took me a whole week to write my first play. It was called "Night of Fear," and it was about a mysterious stranger who visits a family—a mum, a dad, two teenage kids and a lovable grandmother. The stranger pays the family a huge amount of money to stay with them for one night because he says he's in market research and wants to see how a normal family behaves. The stranger has a colleague who is watchful and eerie, which is a good character to have in plays.

At first the stranger seems nice. Then he starts revealing dark secrets about the family. The father is having an affair with the work canteen manager and the mother is sneaking out to seedy nightclubs while the rest of the family is asleep. The son is growing drugs and the daughter is burning down shops. Everyone is stunned. How does the stranger know all these things?

In a highly dramatic moment the stranger announces that he is the Angel of Death and not in market research after all. He has come to collect the grandmother. There's a lot of confrontation because no one wants the grandmother to die. The noise attracts a neighbor, who runs in to see what's going on. The eerie colleague freezes the neighbor with the power of his eyes, and we realize that he too is not in market research. (The part of the neighbor is difficult for an actor, as he must remain perfectly still with his arms in the air for one whole hour.) Eventually the grandmother is dragged away by Death, but only after she reveals that she, too, has a dark secret. She once had a child out of wedlock. The child is the eerie colleague who has gone over to the dark side! People are shocked, the audience claps and the curtain comes down.

I was sure I'd written a masterpiece. Mum and Dad said it was the best play they'd read. When Mum said she'd try to get Will Stretton to stage my play at the SLC, Jack immediately wanted to be in it. Naturally, he wanted to be the main character, Death. He also wanted India to be in the play and said I should add another character, Death's girlfriend. I told Jack that this wouldn't work dramatically. Death wouldn't go round with a girlfriend who looked plastic and smelled of air freshener.

According to the local paper, Mr. Raven (41) was well on the way to tracking down the cyber-terrorist, "following an anonymous tit-off." The letters page had a rather odd letter from an anthropologist. It was his professional opinion that Mr. Raven was a "chromus domus." According to the letter, Mr. Raven showed all the traditional chromus domus characteristics, including a high-domed head and squinty eyes. The name of the anthropologist was Dr. William Shatner.

Next morning, a young local laws officer from the council called around. He told us our nature strip needed cutting back. There were plenty of nature strips in the street that were in worse shape than ours. One of them even had an old telly and a burst settee on it. But the local laws officer said he'd received a complaint about ours alone.

We weren't surprised when Mr. Raven wandered by, as Dad was cutting the grass.

"Hello, Mr. Raven," said Dad. "I suppose you're the one who complained about our nature strip?"

Mr. Raven ignored the question. "I've noticed your letterbox," he said.

"I'm not surprised," said Dad. "It's a magnificent letterbox."

We had the best letterbox in Kinglet, a beautifully constructed thing made of oak and merbau. It looked more like a piece of furniture than a common letterbox. Dad had spent ages on it and was justly proud, even though it was far too ornate for bills and junk mail.

"It sticks out over the footpath," said Mr. Raven. "It's a risk to pedestrians. I suggest you relocate it."

Dad fumed. Mum appeared, sensing there might be trouble.

"Thank you for bringing the matter to our attention," said Mum. "We'll fix it immediately."

"Please do." Mr. Raven left.

"I think he knows you're the cyber-terrorist," Mum said. "He knows you're Dr. William Shatner."

Dad wasn't worried. "He can prove nothing. I covered my tracks."

"He could make life very difficult. I wish you'd stop goading him. It's quite obvious he hates you."

"Not as much as I hate him."

While I did my push-ups and sit-ups in my bedroom that night, I heard Mum and Dad talking downstairs about our upcoming vacation. (Jack and I both have loft bedrooms, so we can hear things that people say anywhere in the house.) We were going to spend two weeks staying in a lodge in the Kruger National Park in South Africa. Neither Jack nor I had ever been out of Australia before. I couldn't wait to get up close to a lion. Jack couldn't wait to buy duty-free skin products.

"Eric, do you really think we should go on safari *every* day?" Mum said. "It's very expensive."

"The boys will love it. And what else is there to do in a national park in South Africa?"

"There's a nice pool at the lodge."

"I'm not going all the way there to sit in a nice pool!"

"We could just spend a few days relaxing."

"It'll be relaxing to look at animals. Unless one of them eats us."

Dad picked up his guitar and started playing "Moonshadow." I waited for Mum to sing along but she didn't, so Dad put down the guitar.

"Zilla, would you miss me if I were eaten up by a savage lion?"

"Of course I would. Would you miss me?"

"How could I? I'd be lion poo."

"I mean if *I* got eaten up by a savage lion and you survived."

"I'd miss you every single day of my life," said Dad. "I'd miss your laughter and your warmth and your long black hairs in the shower."

"Those are *your* hairs," said Mum.

"But do you know what I'd miss most of all?"

"What?"

"Singing 'Moonshadow' with you."

The kids outside were chanting again. Dad raced out into the street. Worried that the kids might chuck stuff at him, I watched from my bedroom window.

“How would you like to make some money?” Dad asked the kids.

They immediately stopped chanting.

“All you have to do is go outside a house and chant ‘Chromedome’ over and over.” Dad gave some money to the biggest kid and told him an address.

I had a fair idea whose address it was.

FACT THREE

Mahatma Gandhi never hurt a fly but still ended up boss of India

The next day, Dad decided not to go to work. This was unusual. He never took sickies. Dad said he had confidential urgent business. Mum took my play to the SLC to see if Will Stretton would stage it. Jack and I went to school.

Sandy Proctor was the only girl in my year who looked anything like Opal Honey. She had big shoulders and biceps because she was a keen swimmer. She also had bleached wavy hair owing to all the chlorine. It stuck out in bunches on either side of her head. Because she had once broken her nose, it was slightly flat, giving her the appearance of a koala. It might seem weird to fancy someone who looks like a marsupial, but I thought Sandy was quite desirable.

During general studies I kept looking across at Sandy Proctor. She had started wearing a sports bra. Sandy realized I was staring at her new bra and she flicked it at the back. I blushed. (When red-haired people blush we really go overboard.) I wasn't sure if Sandy's weird bra-snapping gesture had been intended to put me off or if it were some sort of mating ritual.

After the class, Sandy came over and said she wanted

to see me at lunchtime under the pine trees behind the sports oval. This was where the tough kids hung out, especially a group of girls called Nanky Rats, who went to the Nankeen Shopping Center on weekends to smoke and swear at the shoppers with their babies.

There were six girls smoking under the pine trees. Sandy handed me a cigarette when I arrived. I said I didn't want one because they give you cancer. Two of the girls rolled their eyes, as though cancer were cool. Why had Sandy invited me to join her lunchtime smoking group? Her koala face didn't seem so desirable when she had a cigarette dangling from her lips.

"How come your hair sticks up?" asked Sandy.

I shrugged.

"Would you like to see my bra?" she asked.

The other girls burst out laughing.

"You seemed pretty keen on it before," said Sandy.

I blushed again.

"She likes your brother," said one of the other girls.

That explained it. This was all about Jack.

"Does your brother like me?" asked Sandy.

"I don't know."

"Ask him if he likes me."

Sandy would be the last person Jack would go for, especially as he already had a crush on India, but I told Sandy I'd ask.

"You can go now," said Sandy. "Stop standing there like an ugly dweeb."

•

When Jack and I got home from school we found that Dad had done something unusual to the nature strip. He'd turned it into a vegetable patch.

"I could use some help," said Dad. Perspiration dripped from his forehead. His singlet was soaked.

"You could use a psychiatrist," said Jack.

"Rude gestures!" said Dad.

"Rude gestures to *you*!" Jack walked away into the house.

I changed into old shorts and helped Dad plant his vegetables. I enjoyed playing around in the dirt and couldn't understand why Zoran hated it so much. It was too hot to wear a shirt so I got Dad to rub sunscreen onto my back.

"You're getting broad shoulders," Dad said.

"Not as broad as Opal Honey's," I said. "Dad, do you think I'm an ugly dweeb?"

Dad shook his head. "You're handsome. Just not in a traditional way."

I looked at the brown spots that covered my arms and chest. There were a few on my face as well.

"What about my moles? They're pretty ugly."

"They give you character."

Dad carefully sprinkled seeds into the holes he'd made in the soil, and hummed a Cat Stevens song.

"Girls don't seem to like me much." I wasn't going to tell him about Sandy Proctor and the Nanky Rats.

"You'll meet a girl," said Dad. "You have a good personality and you know lots of interesting facts."

"I don't think interesting facts help you get girls."

"They can." Dad watered his row of freshly sown turnip seeds.

"I don't even know where to *meet* girls," I said. "Not muscular ones like Opal Honey."

"You'll meet them," said Dad. "Though perhaps you shouldn't be so focused on Opal Honey. She probably has to eat a cow a day to build muscles like that. I doubt if she knows any interesting facts at all."

I ignored this insult to my dream woman. "Where did you meet Mum?"

Dad sat on the footpath and rested. "I met your mother at a Cat Stevens concert."

I rested alongside him. "What did you say to Mum? Did you tell her an interesting fact?"

"I'm not proud of this. I thought your mother was so incredibly beautiful, I'd have to say something amazing to impress her."

"What did you say?"

"I told her I knew Cat Stevens."

"That's okay. It's only a white lie."

"It gets worse. I told your mother that if she went out with me, I'd get his autograph for her."

"That's not so good. But I'm sure it's not the only reason Mum went out with you."

"I think it was at first. But then she started to like me. My jokes. My interesting facts. My hair."

"You do have quite good hair."

"And eventually she stopped asking for the autograph. Frankly, I think she knew pretty early on it wasn't going to happen. But I've always felt guilty about it."

This gave me an idea. "Is Cat Stevens still alive?"

"Yes, I believe he is."

"Then why don't you write to him and get his autograph for Mum? If he can write a song as good as 'Moonshadow,' he's obviously a romantic and he'll understand."

Dad winced as sweat from his forehead dribbled into his eye.

"His name isn't Cat Stevens anymore," Dad said. "It's Yusuf Islam. So you see, I can't keep my promise."

"That's a shame."

"It is, Seth. It really is."

Then Dad covered the vegetable patch with a healthy layer of horse manure, the best fertilizer there is.

"What on earth is going on?"

Mum had returned from work. She looked at the former nature strip in disbelief.

"This is your new vegetable patch," Dad smiled. "I've planted basil, beans, turnips and cabbage."

"Eric, did you really take the day off so you could turn our nature strip into a vegetable patch?"

"Yes, I did."

"How could you?"

"Well, I put down some extra top soil and then I used a rake ..."

"You've done this to provoke Mr. Raven."

"I checked the bylaws. It doesn't say anywhere that we can't turn our nature strip into a vegetable garden. There's nothing Mr. Raven can do."

"He'll be round here with a bulldozer, you dingbat!"

"Then I shall lie in front of it. Just as you once did. I always thought you looked very attractive lying in front of bulldozers."

"Don't try to butter me up!" snapped Mum. "I'm furious."

"You shouldn't be. You have a fine vegetable patch."

"You're obsessed with Mr. Raven. It's unhealthy. It's a fight you can't win."

"I can and I will!" said Dad. "Would you like to know an interesting fact, Zilla? It's about Mahatma Gandhi ..."

"I don't care about interesting facts. I don't give two hoots about Mahatma Gandhi. Things are very busy at the Center right now. The state government is threatening to cut funding, the council is giving me a hard time and a little girl was nearly blown away during a kite workshop. You're not helping matters!"

Mum stormed into the house.

"Mum seems to have gone off your interesting facts," I said.

"She's gone off a few other things as well," said Dad, sadly.

I'd noticed the master bedroom hadn't been getting as much use lately.

•

Dr. Penhaligon was our local general practitioner. I always had to take my shirt off when I visited him so he could check my moles.

"You can put your shirt back on now. Your moles are fine," said Dr. Penhaligon.

I pulled on my shirt, working myself up to asking the question that was the real reason for my visit.

"Dr. Penhaligon, I need an aphrodisiac."

Dr. Penhaligon gave me an odd look.

"Do you know what an aphrodisiac is?" he asked.

An aphrodisiac is a potion for making people passionate. I'd learned this from Dad. Unfortunately, a lot of Asian aphrodisiacs are made from bits of endangered species, like pandas. I told Dr. Penhaligon I wanted a panda-friendly one.

"Teenage males don't normally require aphrodisiacs," said Dr. Penhaligon.

"It isn't actually for me. It's for my parents. They don't seem to be as happy with each other as they used to be."

"They told you this?"

"It's pretty obvious. They've been arguing more than ever."

"Well, perhaps they should come and see me."

"Couldn't you just give me something I could slip into their herbal tea?"

"I'm not allowed to do things like that."

"I wouldn't tell anyone."

"What your parents are going through is probably perfectly normal."

"Not for them!"

I explained how Mum and Dad used to run into the master bedroom when Dad played guitar songs.

"Well, it might just be a phase," said Dr. Penhaligon. "Sometimes parents stop being romantic with each other, then rediscover it all over again."

"But how do they rediscover it?"

Dr. Penhaligon's shoulders dropped. "I wish I knew."

I got up to leave but Dr. Penhaligon stopped me for a moment. "Seth, did you say that when your father played songs it had a … passionate effect on your mother?"

"Yes, it did."

He gave me a desperate look. "Can you remember which songs they were?"

Jack had bought himself a new pair of orange tights. He wore them in the drama class and India was impressed. She had, of course, fallen head over heels in love with him. When Will Stretton arrived, we played a trust game where we had to pair off. One person put on a blindfold and the other led them around outside. Jack and India disappeared in the long grass down by the river. I led Tyrone around but didn't give him clear enough directions and he walked into a bike rack. Tyrone was very good about it. He said it didn't hurt that much, though I could tell it did. Casper led Jasper straight into the ladies' toilets where they had a fight with liquid soap, which we discovered is quite dangerous if it gets into the eyes.

At the end of the class Will held up "Night of Fear."

"Seth has written a play," said Will. "And I intend to stage it here at the Center."

I knew the play was good so it didn't surprise me, but I was still rapt. Tyrone gave a little clap. He was easily the nicest person in the class.

"Congratulations, Seth," said Will. "You've written a fine first draft."

"First draft?"

"It isn't ready yet," said Will. "You'll need to rewrite it."

Of course the play was ready. But I pretended Will was right. "You may even have to do *two* more drafts," said Will.

"I understand."

I wasn't going to change a word of my masterpiece.

"Can I be in it?" asked either Casper or Jasper.

"Not if you keep doing that with your finger," said Will.

"What's the play about?" asked Poppy.

"Death," I said.

"Death is unlucky," Nangret said.

"Do many people die?" asked Casper or Jasper.

"Only one," I said.

The twins looked disappointed.

"But someone is painfully frozen."

The twins were keen again.

"Does anybody have anything else they'd like to contribute to the class?" asked Will Stretton.

Poppy said she wanted to read out her latest poem, and started before anyone could say anything.

"Seagulls with feathers covered in oil,
Plastic bags and bits of foil,
Dolphins caught in a fishing net,
Things like this make me quite upset.
Toilets flowing into the sea,
Why do such things have to be?
There just doesn't seem to be any solution
To this really terrible thing that we call pollution."

Poppy wept. So did Casper. Jasper had stuck a compass in him.

I went into the kitchenette to rehydrate, which is health jargon for drinking water. I turned on the tap too hard and rehydrated my tights. As I wiped the water off with a tea towel, I noticed a copy of *Dolly* magazine on the bench top.

I picked up the magazine, sat down and started reading. There were articles about slimming, sexy swimwear and the tragedy of anorexia. There was a column where girls sent in stories about their boyfriends. They seemed made up. Would a boy really be so stupid as to fix his broken sunglasses with superglue then put them on before the glue dried so they stuck to his face?

There was an article called "22 Ways to Know If He Is Mr. Right." It was a list compiled by leading psychologists. This could come in handy. I didn't have much idea about what girls really wanted. All I knew was that they wanted my brother and that was no help to me at all. I tore out the page and tucked it down my tights.

Six pages were taken up by a muscular trio of girls modeling underwear. They didn't look skinny, like most models. They were Olympians. I tore these pages out, too, and stuffed them into my tights.

There was an advice page called "Dolly Doctor." One girl was worried that her breasts weren't the same size as each other. According to "Dolly Doctor," this was common and normal.

"Hi," someone said. "What are you doing?"

I looked up to see a tall, fit-looking girl wearing gym shorts and a tank top. She was about my age. She had green eyes and long straight brown hair and she was sweating. She was the closest thing to Opal Honey I'd ever seen and I felt my knees go weak. I said the first thing that came into my head.

"I was just reading about wheatgrass."

I closed the magazine so the girl wouldn't know I'd been reading about breasts.

"What's wheatgrass?" she asked.

"It's health stuff. My mum drinks it."

"It's weird to drink grass."

"She turns it into juice," I said. "With a juicer. She says it's good for her chee."

"What's that?"

"I think it's an internal organ."

The girl rehydrated, rinsed her glass and put it away. I'd never seen anyone rinse a glass so perfectly.

"Which class are you doing?" I asked. She was sweating so much, I guessed it wasn't one of the arty ones or fish care.

“Kickboxing,” said the girl.

Kickboxing had only just been introduced at the Center. Kids had requested it but Mum had been reluctant because she thought kickboxing was violent. Dad reassured her that there were two types of kickboxing: cardio and combat. Cardio was nonviolent and for exercise only. Dad had done it himself when he was a teenager. Mum was eventually persuaded.

“I didn’t know there were any girls in the kickboxing class,” I said.

“There’s just one.”

“You,” I said idiotically.

The girl nodded. “Me.”

I cursed myself for not signing up for kickboxing. I’d presumed the class would be nothing but thugs, not perfect specimens of feminine strength like the girl before me.

“Which class are *you* doing?” she asked.

“Drama.”

“Do you want to be an actor?”

“Not really. I could never be a film actor. My eyes don’t come out properly in photos. I’d only ever be able to play androids.”

“You do have unusual eyes.”

“My gran has them. She says they let you see into the soul.”

“Do they?”

“No, my gran’s mad.”

“What happened to your tights?”

I looked down at the wet patch on my tights.

"I wet myself. With the tap. It's too sensitive. I'll have to tell Mum."

"Why will you tell your mum?"

"She runs this place."

By now the girl had probably noticed how my eyes kept straying toward her arms; wonderful brown arms with well-formed triceps. Here she was admiring my eyes while I was gazing longingly at her upper arms. Perhaps Sandy Proctor was right and I was a dweeb after all.

The girl moved toward the door. She turned to look at me before leaving. I'm pretty sure she checked out my arms.

"What's your name?" the girl asked.

"Seth."

The girl frowned as though this wasn't the correct answer. "What sort of name is that?"

"He was an Egyptian god." This sounded boastful so I added, "He murdered his brother."

"I'm Miranda," the girl said.

Even her name was perfect. "That's a moon," I said.

"I know."

"It's around Uranus."

"I know. There's another one called Ariel."

"I prefer your name to mine. I'd much rather be a moon than a murderer."

"Me, too. But your name is okay."

Miranda smiled, picked up the *Dolly* and walked off.

My heart sank. I didn't realize the *Dolly* was hers. She was bound to browse through it and realize that some perve had pulled out the underwear pages. She'd work out that the perve was me. She'd probably already noticed the curious lumps in my tights. Why did life have to play such rotten tricks? I'd just met the most sensational girl in the world—and I was wearing tights. Wet tights with curious lumps. I tried to recall our conversation and how many stupid things I'd said. There were at least two.

After meeting Miranda I was convinced that she was everything I wanted. She had great arms and she knew about moons. I wanted to be her Mr. Right. After such a bad beginning, I had my work cut out.

FACT FOUR

The Kia parrot in New Zealand is the only parrot in the world that enjoys rolling in snow

Mum and Dad were delighted that Will Stretton had decided to put on my play. We celebrated with a bottle of red wine bought from Kinglet market. It seemed to contain grasshoppers as well as grapes. Dad said there was nothing wrong with drinking wine, provided we didn't become alcoholics or Liberal voters. Mum served up some Kinglet market goat's cheese that tasted far too goaty.

"Here's to you, Seth," toasted Mum. "Congratulations on your play."

We all had a few mouthfuls of the wine.

"And here's to me," said Jack.

"Why you?' I said.

"I asked India to marry me and she accepted."

He'd do anything for attention.

"You're too young to get married," said Mum.

"It'll be a long engagement," said Jack.

Dutifully, we toasted Jack's future marriage to India.

Mum offered around the crumbly white goat's cheese. Jack pushed it away.

"I've discovered something interesting about myself," said Jack. "I'm lactose intolerant." (Jack had suffered from many ailments in his time, mostly fictitious. Once Jack complained that he'd lost all feeling in his feet. Mum and Dad were concerned. They took him to Dr. Penhaligon, who promptly stuck a pin in Jack's foot. Jack yelled out and Dr. Penhaligon told him, "Well, we seem to have fixed that problem.")

"Jack, how do you know you're lactose intolerant?" Dad asked.

"I tried an experiment on myself. I drank a liter of milk and I felt sick."

"Most people would feel sick after drinking a whole liter of milk," said Mum.

"I still think I should avoid milk products. India says she's lactose intolerant, too. Milk gives her mucus."

"Well, mucus is important," said Dad. "If we didn't have mucus, the acids inside us would dissolve our own stomachs."

As interesting facts go, I thought this was a pretty good one, but Mum told Dad not to be gross. I poured some more wine for Mum and Dad. In the old days, red wine would have put my parents in a romantic mood. Even red wine that tasted of grasshoppers. I figured that if I got them just a bit drunk and Dad started playing Cat Stevens on his guitar, they might even race off to the master bedroom. Dad gave Mum a "Moonshadow" look as he downed his second glass. Mum said the wine was giving her a headache and emptied hers onto the garden.

Later that evening the possums mated noisily outside my window.

•

Thinking of Miranda with her green eyes and her well-developed arms, I put the Mr. Right list up on my bedroom wall next to the picture of Opal Honey. (There's a copy of the list at the back of this book in Appendix II.) Opal Honey no longer seemed so beautiful, now that I'd met Miranda. She looked too shiny. Her quads were bigger than necessary. Her toothy grin was nowhere near as alluring as the wonderful smile Miranda had given me when she'd told me that Seth was an okay name.

History had taught me that Miranda would probably prefer my little brother to me because he was so handsome. However, I now had a secret weapon. I had a list compiled by leading psychologists. All I had to do was keep Miranda away from Jack and try out all the things on the list. She might think I was Mr. Right. It was worth a shot.

The first Mr. Right rule was: *He takes an interest in your hobbies and pastimes.*

"I'd like to do the kickboxing course," I announced to Mum and Dad, who were washing the dishes.

"You'll have to wait for the next one," said Mum. "You can't join a course halfway through."

"I know a bit about cardio-kickboxing," said Dad. "I could teach Seth."

Mum didn't look too keen. She siphoned the water out of the sink and into a bucket so it could be used to wash the car. (Our car was never really clean and often had bits of food on it.)

"I'll teach you how to do jumpkicks," said Dad. He threw a plate in the air and caught it, to prove how nimble he was. Then he dropped it. "Oops! Shouldn't have had that second glass of wine."

Mum made far too much fuss. It was just a stupid plate.

Mr. Raven visited first thing the next morning. Mum made sure to stay close to Dad when he answered the door.

"I'd like a word about the nature strip," said Mr. Raven.

Dad played innocent again. "Is there a problem?"

"There have been numerous complaints about the smell."

Ever the peacemaker, Mum cut in. "Mr. Raven, perhaps you'd like a mango *lassi*?"

"What is a mango *lassi*, Mrs. Parrot?"

"It's an Indian drink made with yogurt."

"In that case, I would *not* like a mango *lassi*."

"Have you seen the nature strip three doors up?" Dad asked Mr. Raven.

"I'm not interested in the nature strip three doors up."

"They appear to be growing old armchairs," said Dad. "There were two there last week, and I observed another one yesterday. They all stink."

"They're of no concern to me, Mr. Parrot."

"I just wondered why you're so upset about our nice new vegetable patch when a disgusting old armchair patch appears to be growing out of control just three doors up."

"We're sorry about the vegetable garden," said Mum. "We'll get rid of it if people are upset by it."

Dad was about to say something but Mum trod on his toe.

"Thank you, Mrs. Parrot," said Mr. Raven. "I'm glad we see eye to eye on this issue."

Mr. Raven left with his clipboard.

"That hurt," Dad complained to Mum, nursing a sore toe.

"You're lucky," said Mum. "I nearly punched you in the nose."

Mum made mango *lassis* for us all, except Jack, who was lactose intolerant for the time being.

"Will you please remove that vegetable garden today?" Mum asked Dad.

He shook his head. "I'd have to take another day off work. They wouldn't be too happy about that. I'll do it on the weekend."

"Promise?"

Dad sighed. "In the old days you'd have stood up to that mean old coot!"

Mum had a big *lassi* moustache on her top lip. "Eric, did you ever stop to think what'd happen if Mr. Raven and some of his colleagues decided to gang up against the Center? You know there are people on the council who don't like us. They could probably close us down if they put their minds to it."

"They wouldn't dare. You have the backing of the state government."

"You also have a moustache," said Jack.

"It suits you," said Dad.

Mum wiped it off, unamused.

"You'd have laughed at that once," said Dad.

"Stop talking about the old days, Eric. Things are different now."

I took the day off school and got rid of the vegetable patch all on my own, without telling Dad. It seemed an act of vandalism, but I wanted to get Mr. Raven out of our life.

When Dad got home, he was disappointed to see that the nature strip was now just a raked patch of earth, scattered with grass seeds I'd bought from the nursery with my pocket money. The pigeons were already getting stuck into the seeds.

"I'm sorry about the vegetable patch, Dad."

"That's all right, Seth."

Dad gave me some extra pocket money to show that there were no hard feelings.

After dinner, Dad went out to the backyard to pee on the lemon tree. He always did this, as it was good for the tree. I peed alongside him. We zipped ourselves up.

"Come and sit with me," I said. We both sat cross-legged on the couch grass.

"I think it's about time you and I had a talk about relationships," I said.

"Sure. Are you having problems, Seth?"

"I'm more concerned about *your* relationship."

Dad was thrown. "Oh."

"I've been worried about you and Mum lately. I think you may be drifting apart."

"Why do you say that?"

"You don't seem to get along as well as you used to. You hardly ever laugh together. It bothers me. I've even tried to seek expert advice."

"You have?"

"Yes."

"What have you found out?"

"Nothing. I'll have to do more seeking."

"Your mother and I are just going through a rough patch."

"I think it has something to do with Mr. Raven."

Dad bristled. "I hate that man!"

I agreed. "He's horrible."

We sat in silence for a few moments. There was a shooting star. I wished for Miranda to be my serious girlfriend. Dad must have picked up on my thoughts.

"Are there any nice girls in the drama class?" he asked.

"There's one called Poppy. She's nice, but she's thin and her poetry's dreadful. And there's Nangret, but she's bonkers as well as thin."

"You can't keep discounting girls because they don't look like Opal Honey."

"I did meet one girl. She does the kickboxing course."

Dad smiled. “I thought so.”

“I got off to a bad start with her. I desecrated her *Dolly*.”

“That sounds serious.”

“I’m trying to work out how to impress her.”

“Don’t try too hard. Girls don’t like that. Just be yourself.”

“That hasn’t worked so far.”

“It will.” Dad gazed up at the heavens again. I expected him to point out some constellations, but he just sighed.

“I hope everything is okay with you and Mum,” I said. “Maybe going to Africa will help.”

“I’m sure it will, Seth.”

That night I dreamed of jumpkicking with Miranda on the vast plains of the Serengeti in Africa. It was the best dream of my life, until white hunters came along and shot us full of darts. The chief white hunter looked exactly like Mr. Raven.

In Arizona, Opal Honey was found guilty of taking human growth hormones and banned from the Ms. Olympia contests for life.

FACT FIVE

The longest recorded flight of a chicken is thirteen seconds

I took down the disgraced Opal Honey from my bedroom wall. With Opal gone, I could focus on the Mr. Right list. The third rule on the list was: *He takes pride in his appearance.* I already took pride in my physique and exercised daily. My problem was my hair.

I asked Jack if I could borrow his hair products. He had about a thousand of them in his room, along with dozens of fluffy stuffed animals, all gifts from India. The biggest was a pink elephant called Mr. Banerjee. Neither Mum nor Dad approved of the cuddly toys, as many of them were made in overseas sweatshops. But Jack treasured them because they were from his future wife, so he was allowed to keep them.

Jack said his hair products would be wasted on my bright red frizz and that I needed a whole new haircut. He told me to go to Franca's Hair, and not Mr. Wedd the local barber who had the shakes from his home brew. Then Jack stuck out his tongue. There was a silver stud right in the middle of it.

"You got your tongue pierced!"

"Yes," said Jack.

"I thought you were going to get a stud in your ear."

"I was."

"Did they miss?"

"I decided on this instead."

I'd seen plenty of tongue studs before. The Nanky Rats all had them. Even Mr. Kenvyn, my schoolteacher, had one, though he was going through a mid-life crisis because he also had contact lenses the color of Windex. But I couldn't cope with the idea of Jack with a piece of metal in his mouth that wasn't there for medical reasons.

"You're insane," I said.

"You're Nicole Kidman."

"Don't call me that."

"Well, don't call me insane."

"Does it hurt?"

Jack shook his head.

"Can you eat with it?"

Jack rolled his eyes like a Nanky Rat. "You saw me eating tonight. Why are you asking so many stupid questions?"

"I'm in shock. Mum and Dad will be, too."

"Don't tell them."

"They'll find out, you idiot. Why did you do it?"

"To be an individual. India's got one, too. All her friends have. And when I went to get the tongue piercing, I got this as well."

Jack started to undo his belt.

"Stop!" I yelled.

Jack handed the belt to me.

"The buckle," said Jack. "I got a new belt buckle."

Franca the hairdresser had dyed blonde hair. She also had a bubbly personality and a big bust. I could see why Jack liked her so much. It was because of the bust.

There was only one customer in the salon when I arrived. She was covered in a plastic poncho and seated under one of those pedestal dryers, up the back. All I could see of the woman was that she was reading a copy of *Ralph* magazine. *Ralph* is sort of like *Dolly*, except it's for men. *Ralph* doesn't have psychologists.

"So you're Jack's brother?" said Franca. "He's a little cutie."

"Yes, he's adorable." Just once it would have been nice to meet someone who didn't think Jack was heaven on a stick. "Can you make my hair look like his?"

Franca frowned as she studied my profile. "I don't think it would suit you. Your face is the wrong shape. This style would be better." Franca pointed to a photo on the wall. It was of a man with a strange haircut that had a veranda out the front. I told her I thought the man looked thuggish.

"That's my boyfriend, Vincenzo," said Franca.

"Actually, he's quite handsome," I said.

"Do you like that haircut?"

"Not really."

"Do you have a girlfriend?"

"No."

"If you let me cut your hair like that, you will get a girlfriend."

"Then go right ahead."

Franca started giving me a Vincenzo haircut. I asked her about her home country. Was she from the north or the south of Italy? Franca said she was from Albury. Her dad still lived there but her mum had moved to Gang Gang after the divorce.

"My parents are having a few marital problems of their own," I said.

"Well, divorce isn't the end of the world. Things'll work out. That's what the Italians say."

It probably sounded better in Italian.

The phone rang and Franca answered it. Soon she was having a huge argument with the person at the other end of the line. I pretended not to notice, which was difficult because Franca kept walking around kicking things. I don't speak Italian but some words like *bastardo* are easy to translate. Then Franca slammed down the receiver. I asked her if everything was all right and she said yes. Franca picked up the scissors and snipped away angrily.

"Did you get some bad news?" I asked.

"Yes," said Franca.

She didn't want to talk about it and I couldn't think of anything else to say. It was weird having a silent haircut. Mr. Wedd always talked his head off when he cut my hair. He talked about horse racing and ferrets and his awful family in New Zealand. But Franca snipped and snipped without a word. I let out a yelp as she nicked my earlobe.

"I'm so sorry!" Franca cried.

"That's all right."

"It's not all right. I have cut your ear. That's a terrible thing for a hairdresser to do."

"It's only a little cut. My ear won't fall off."

It was starting to bleed and Franca gave me a towel to hold against it. She was getting worked up. "I should kill myself."

"Please don't kill yourself. Not now."

"I'm sorry, I can't cut your hair today."

"But you've already started."

"I'll give you an angry haircut. I might hurt your ear again."

I was desperate. "Can someone else do it?"

"I'm the only one here today." Franca burst into tears, then revealed the awful truth. "Vincenzo just dumped me."

"I'm sorry," I said. "But you'll find someone else. You have to get on with life. You'll meet new people. Please finish cutting my hair."

"I'll kill Vincenzo," Franca said. "With these scissors I will kill him."

"Could you finish my hair first?"

"I'll do it later, after I have killed Vincenzo."

Franca stomped to the back of the salon. She turned off the pedestal dryer and tilted it up to reveal that the woman was in fact Zoran. He looked startled when he saw me there. He had bits of silver foil in his hair that would have caused a few raised eyebrows in Serbia.

"Hello, Set," said Zoran. "I am just getting streaks. My wife make me do it."

"That's okay, Zoran," I said.

"We are lucky to live in Australia where men can be streaky. In Serbia if you are streaky they make you do military service in defective submarines. Franca, you will take the metal papers off now, yes?"

"I'm sorry, Zoran. I have to go. I'm closing the shop."

"What? But my hair is like Christmas tree."

I explained to Zoran. "Franca's boyfriend's left her and now she wants to kill him."

"Finish my hair and I will help you to kill him," said Zoran.

Franca shook her head.

"I cannot go home like this," said Zoran. "My wife will not like it. She hate Christmas trees."

Franca told us we both had to leave, so she could go to murder Vincenzo with scissors.

"Make sure you murder him good," said Zoran. He ran over to his Commodore and drove off. I got on my bike.

Mr. Wodd had already started on his home brew when I arrived, and he just laughed when he saw what Franca had done. We had a serious shortage of well-adjusted haircutters in Kinglet. Perhaps it was something I could do to make serious money when I was older.

Dad was out in the garden peeing on the lemon tree again, even though it was broad daylight. Quiet, retiring Mr. Robbins was next door, showing off his garden to his dear old silver-haired mother. I thought it was wrong for

Dad to pee so close to an old lady, even if she wouldn't be able to see what he was doing.

"Where have you been?" Dad asked.

I was miserable. "The hairdresser's."

"What sort of haircut is that?"

"Franca didn't finish it."

"It doesn't look that bad." It was nice of Dad to lie. "It doesn't look that good, either. Maybe I could fix it up for you."

Dad touched a few strands of my hair and rearranged them to see if there was anything he could do. I didn't really want Dad touching my hair after he'd touched his penis. When I told him, he was understanding and not at all offended.

"Why don't I show you how to do jumpkicks?" Dad suggested.

I shook my head. "I'm too depressed."

Dad quoted his hero, Merlin the Magician. "'There's nothing better for being sad than to learn something.'"

Dad had made a special pad to wear on his hand. I practiced kicking the pad as he kept holding it higher.

"Come on, Seth! You're not trying!"

"I'm worried I might kick your head in."

"You won't. I know what I'm doing. Start from more of a crouch. Move your hips, like this."

I tried to follow Dad's instructions, and he held the pad even higher.

Jack saw us and joined in, yelling "Wahhh!" He was

wearing nothing but his orange tights. Soon we were both doing jumpkicks like Asian movie stars.

"Jack, let Seth have a go on his own," Dad said. "It's difficult when you're both coming at me."

But Jack wouldn't do what he was told. He never did. So I stopped jumping and let Jack take over.

Next door, Mr. Robbins was showing off his camellias to his mother. She was more interested in the jumpkicks going on in our backyard. She wandered over to have a closer look. Mum also watched from the back landing. The bellbirds went *ping!*

Jack did a particularly high kick and split his tights right down the middle. He wasn't wearing any underwear. It took Jack a few moments to realize that he was exposed for all the world to see. Sweet old ladies are not supposed to laugh at things like this, but Mr. Robbins's mother cackled so hard she nearly had a heart attack. Dad and I were soon rolling on the grass, guffawing.

Jack covered up his rude bits and ran back into the house. Mum wasn't laughing at all. This was high-class comedy but she didn't even have a smirk on her face. Back in the twentieth century, she'd have roared with laughter.

The next drama class was tomorrow. I'd probably be seeing Miranda again. I had the stupidest haircut in the world and didn't look like the sort of man who takes pride in his appearance. Franca's Hair was still closed, probably because Franca was in prison.

I looked for other things on the Mr. Right list that might

make up for my half a haircut. The second thing was: *He gives thoughtful and inventive presents.* I tried to think of thoughtful and inventive presents to give Miranda.

I kept thinking about it all through school the next day, while Mr. Kenvyn taught the class about continental drift. Maybe Miranda would like an atlas? No, that wasn't thoughtful or inventive. That was boring and tragic. That was a Mr. Wrong present.

"What were the countries called before they split up?"

It took me a few moments to realize Mr. Kenvyn was talking to me.

"Pardon?"

Windex-eyes fixed me with a stare. "Are you paying attention, Seth?"

"Yes, Mr. Kenvyn."

"Then can you tell me what the countries were called before they split up?"

"Happily married," I said, and kids laughed.

If Mr. Kenvyn could have frozen me with the power of his eyes, he would have. But they didn't teach people things like that at teacher's college.

"The answer is Gondwanaland," said Mr. Kenvyn. "Please concentrate and stop gazing out the window."

"Yes. Sorry, Mr. Kenvyn."

He continued with the class and I continued gazing out the window. I saw something that gave me an idea for a thoughtful and inventive present.

•

In the drama class that afternoon we settled down to read my play. Will Stretton gave the role of Death to Tyrone. I didn't want Tyrone to play Death because I didn't think Death should be overweight. When you think of the Grim Reaper you don't picture a fat man in tights. But I didn't say anything.

The parts of the mother and the father went to Jack and India. They started cuddling each other to get into character. Will Stretton told them if they didn't stop he'd chuck them out of the class. Poppy got the grandmother part. Nangret was the neighbor. She said she didn't want to play a frozen man. Will said it was important for actors to be challenged. He himself had once been a carrot, though it was in a TV ad, not a play. Quiet Lukas was given the job of reading the stage directions. When he started, we had to explain that we wanted him to read them *out loud.*

The play reading went for thirty minutes, not the two hours I'd expected. Tyrone was seriously creepy as Death. He was such a good actor that you forgot about his plumpness. Poppy was good as the grandmother, too. Because my play had run so short, we were left with a lot of time to fill. Poppy took out her latest poem. She said that it had been inspired by my play and that it was highly symbolic.

"Once I climbed a building high,
Lots of people I did spy,
In the streets and in the roads,

Carrying quite heavy loads,
All of them looked sad to me,
Sad as sad as sad could be,
Wandering through street and lane,
Dressed in clothes that looked rather plain,
'Come to me!' I told them all,
'Join me on my building tall!'
But they didn't hear my cry,
They just went home to die."

When Poppy finished reading, she asked if she could read out another one but Will Stretton told her there was no time. We finished the drama class early.

I crept over to the room where they do the kickboxing. There was Miranda in a singlet, doing the best jump-kicks. She was a miracle in motion. The teacher, Mr. Quong, was tiny and at least fifty. He was so quick and nimble, I could understand why Asian children were so respectful to their elders. If they were anything like Mr. Quong, elderly Chinese people could really kick butt.

I went to wait in the kitchen so that I could give Miranda my thoughtful and inventive present.

When Miranda arrived she was sweating profusely, which made her more attractive.

"What happened to your hair?" she asked.

"I was involved in a freak hairdressing accident."

"Oh." Miranda rehydrated magnificently.

"I saw you in the kickboxing class," I said. "I'm interested in kickboxing, but my mum won't let me do it." This sounded pathetic, so I added, "She doesn't want me to start a course halfway through."

"My dad doesn't even know I'm here," said Miranda.

"Why not?"

"It's easier if I don't tell him everything."

"He should be proud. You're the best one in the class."

"I'm not."

"*I* think you are." I hadn't bothered to look at anyone else in the class. They could have been baboons in hats for all I knew.

"I've got a present for you," I said.

I reached into the fridge and took out the container I'd left there earlier. I'd bought it from the health-food shop across the road from school. Miranda blinked. Had I made a mistake? Was this a dumb present? Was it worse than an atlas?

"What is it?"

"Wheatgrass. You seemed interested."

Miranda smiled. "Wheatgrass. I remember."

I realized that I was no longer staring at Miranda's arms. My eyes had moved to her chest. This was not Mr. Right behavior. I started looking at everything in the kitchenette that wasn't Miranda's chest. Suddenly the dish rack became fascinating. What should I talk about? Not dish racks.

"The ancient Aztecs thought wheatgrass would make them live forever," I said. "They were wrong."

My eyes were straying again. I focused on the coffee-stained benchtop, where I'd first spied Miranda's magazine.

"I'm sorry about your *Dolly*," I said. "Some of the pages fell out when I was flipping through it."

"I didn't find the article about wheatgrass."

"Those were probably the pages that fell out."

"It must have been a big article."

"It was quite big, yes."

Miranda knew where the pages had gone. I'd have to honor the Mr. Right list. I'd have to tell the truth.

"I'm sorry," I said. "I didn't know it was your *Dolly* or I wouldn't have removed the pages. And even though there were pictures of girls, they were tasteful. You see, I'm interested in muscles."

"So am I," said Miranda.

I was delighted. "I may even be a muscle doctor one day. Possibly a reflexologist."

This was sort of true. I had no idea what I'd be, so why not a reflexologist?

"I'll give the pages back," I said.

"No, that's fine. You can keep them."

Miranda put her glass away.

"Where do you live?" I asked.

"Gang Gang."

I'd always thought it was the stupidest name a town could have. But the way Miranda said "Gang Gang" made it seem like a magical place.

"Where do *you* live?" Miranda asked.

"Singlet."

"What?"

"I mean Kinglet."

The wonderful herbal smell that Miranda gave off was driving me crazy. I asked her what perfume she was wearing. She told me it was Dencorub. I was feeling dizzy and I knew that if I didn't pop the question now I never would.

"Would you like to get together sometime?"

Miranda probably had boys hitting on her all the time. And they would have been better-looking boys than I was.

"What did you have in mind?" she asked.

"We could go to the Earthlight Festival this Saturday. Unless you'd like to do something else. Like bushwalking or abseiling or something. Not that I know how to abseil. But I'd be prepared to learn. Or we could hire a kayak. Do you like kayaks?"

"Sorry," said Miranda. "I'm orienteering in the foothills on Saturday. Maybe some other time?"

She was gone. The smell of Dencorub lingered in the air. There were so many things I'd wanted to ask Miranda, but my brain had let me down. Which were her favorite muscles? Did she do her push-ups from the knees or the toes? Did she have a mesomorphic body-type or was she ectomorphic like me?

Even though I'd asked Miranda none of these important questions, it was wonderful to think that she was taking home the wheatgrass I'd bought her.

•

On the way back to Jacana Avenue, I noticed that two nature strips had been turned into vegetable gardens. Dad had started a trend.

Franca had not murdered Vincenzo after all, and had reopened her salon. She fixed my hair for free. She made it straighter, and gave me a veranda.

"Now you will get a girlfriend," she said. "You look *belissimo*."

Franca was in a good mood. She and Vincenzo were back together. She told me he'd given her a wonderful present. When I asked what it was, Franca said, "Come with me."

She took me through a door at the back of the salon, into a room that smelled of fresh paint. Pictures of rain forests hung on the wall. There were two chaise longues draped with elegant Indian cloth. There was a mirror and a lamp made of salt crystal. As I walked into the room, Franca flicked a switch and harp music came out of two speakers mounted on the ceiling. It was a peaceful, private place. A sanctuary.

"This is the beauty room," said Franca. "This is where I will wax ladies. I always wanted a room like this. From now on, I won't just be Franca's Hair. I'll be Franca's Hair and Legs."

"Wasn't this room always here?"

"It was just a nasty old store room. After our fight, Vincenzo came in here with paint and plaster. It took him a week to do all this." So that's why the salon had been closed.

"Not a bad present, eh?" said Franca. "Not a bad boyfriend."

The beauty room was thoughtful and inventive. Franca was Vincenzo's again. The *Dolly* psychologists really knew their stuff.

On the way home I stopped in at Mr. Ha's pharmacy. Mr. Ha was one of those chemists who likes to be just a bit too helpful.

"I'd like a tube of Dencorub, please," I said.

"What is the Dencorub for?" asked Mr. Ha.

"I have an injury," I lied.

"Where is the injury?"

"In the head."

"Whereabouts in the head?"

"Near my eyes."

"Well, you shouldn't put Dencorub near your eyes."

"I also have a sore latissimus dorsi."

Mr. Ha was so surprised when I mentioned this back muscle, that he fetched the Dencorub without further comment.

"There's something else I need." Now was the right time to make use of Mr. Ha's habit of being overhelpful. "Mr. Ha, what product would you recommend as an aphrodisiac?"

"I certainly wouldn't recommend Dencorub," said Mr. Ha.

He went off to serve a customer who had come in and wanted shampoo.

"The correct way to use shampoo is to wet your hair first," Mr. Ha explained overhelpfully to the customer.

Mum and Dad said my new haircut made me look like a male model. Jack said it made me look like a male prostitute.

"Rude gestures!" I said to Jack.

"Rude gestures to *you*!"

I crept off to my bedroom with my tube of Dencorub and guiltily sat there sniffing. Then I rubbed some of it on my rhomboideus major to see how it felt. It was brilliant. No wonder Miranda used so much of the stuff.

After dinner I wandered out to the backyard with Dad to pee on the lemon tree again. Mosquitoes sang in my ears.

"You smell unusual," said Dad.

"It's Dencorub."

"Are you hurt?"

"Just a bit stiff."

We both started to pee.

"How are things with your kickboxing girl?"

"I'm taking things slowly. I gave her some grass and she seemed quite pleased."

"Grass?"

"Wheatgrass, not marijuana."

"Oh, I see."

"And how's it going with Mum?" I asked.

"She's very busy at the moment, preparing for the

Earthlight Festival."

"How are things on the romantic front?"

"Fairly quiet, Seth."

"I tried to seek advice from Mr. Ha today," I said.

"Seth, I appreciate your efforts, but it might be better if you leave this one to your mother and me."

"Okay."

"You're not offended?"

"No."

"You sound as though you're in pain."

I was.

"It's physical pain, not mental pain," I said.

"What's the matter?"

My penis was stinging.

"Dad, I seem to have Dencorub on my fingers."

"And you've touched your penis?"

"Of course I have! It's very difficult to pee at something without touching your penis."

I could tell Dad was trying to stifle a laugh.

"It's not funny! It hurts!"

"I'm sorry. Go in the shower and wash it off."

"Dad, please don't tell Jack about this or everyone at school will know."

"Of course I won't tell him. Now off you go."

The pain began to subside and I relaxed.

"Actually it's calmed down now."

"I'm pleased to hear it."

I managed to put my penis back into my pants without touching it again.

"I guess it is pretty funny," I said.

Dad chuckled. "Yes."

We wandered back into the house. Mum had been watching us from the kitchen window.

"Eric, do you really have to pee on the lemon tree?" Mum asked, putting dishes away.

Dad was a little surprised.

"Lemon trees need nitrogen, and there's nitrogen in human pee. It's common sense."

"We *do* have a perfectly good dual-flush toilet, you know."

"Of course I know," said Dad. "I helped install it."

Mum said nothing. I nearly told her about my experience with the Dencorub. I was desperate for her to laugh again. But I thought it best to keep the Dencorub story a secret between Dad and me.

That night I didn't sleep well and had another weird dream about Miranda. The two of us were in a huge field of wheatgrass. And just when the dream started to get interesting, a black flapping creature swooped down from a cloudless sky. It was the Angel of Death and it had the face of Mr. Raven.

FACT SIX

Tea-tree oil is good for ant bites

African drums were playing. Someone dressed in a pig costume with a cape threw a bucket of silver confetti at me then wickedly scurried away. The Phantom Pig appeared every year at the Earthlight Festival. No one knew who was inside the costume. It was one of life's great mysteries.

The Earthlight Festival was an annual Kinglet event, held on the sports oval. The local paper described it as "a nun-filled celebration of health and alternative medicine." Mum and Dad were hard at work helping to run the day. Jack was there with India. I'd come alone. After my sleepless night, the bright morning sunlight hurt my eyes.

There was a bouncy castle and a merry-go-round and dozens of stalls devoted to alternative medicine and therapies. There were probably love potions, but I honored Dad's request and didn't make inquiries.

I wondered what Miranda was doing now, while I was walking around looking at hippies and the bouncy castle. Was she still asleep or was she already orienteering in the foothills, her calf muscles bulging and her lustrous brown hair plastered to a forehead dripping with sweat? Maybe she was applying Dencorub to her trapezius?

At the falafel tent I bumped into Poppy from the drama class.

"You look lost," she said.

"Just thinking about my play." I was actually thinking about Miranda's trapezius.

"I think it's a good play," said Poppy. "I like the grandmother. I hope I play her in the production."

"You're a good actor. You probably will."

"What made you write the play? Did your grandma die?"

I shook my head. "It's just a bunch of stuff I made up."

"When my grandpa died I wrote a poem about it. I learned it off by heart so I could say it at the funeral."

And she went right ahead and said it.

"Grandpa, though you've gone away,
Still we think of you today,
With your walking stick and hat,
You were nice and not at all fat,
People liked the stories you told,
And the way you would hardly ever scold,
You will live inside our hearts,
And you were fairly good at darts,
'Do they play darts in heaven?' I cry,
'Will your darts hit someone in the …'"

"Would you like a falafel?" I interrupted.

Poppy said yes. I bought her three falafels because I thought she should bulk up.

Poppy and I walked around together for a bit. It was only ten o'clock in the morning and you could already smell marijuana smoke in the air. It was a common enough smell in Kinglet. Poppy asked me if I'd ever tried marijuana and I told her it gives you brain damage. Poppy said her father smoked it all the time and she agreed with me.

A clown in a green fright wig came up to us. It was my mother, carrying a bucket of coins. Every year she and Dad helped to organize the festival. I introduced Poppy to Mum and put two dollars in Mum's bucket. I didn't know what cause I was supporting. It might have been the brown boobies.

"Have you seen your father?" Mum asked.

"No."

"Do you have sunscreen on?"

"Yes, Mum."

"On your nose?"

"Yes, Mum."

"And your ears?"

"Yes, Mum."

"What about your legs?"

It was embarrassing to be treated like a moronic child who'd never heard of skin cancer. Before Mum could think of any other parts of my body that might need sunscreen, I told her that Poppy and I had to move on because some friends were waiting for us. This is what you say when you want to get away from someone.

"If you see your father, tell him he's needed at the front gate. It was nice to meet you, Poppy."

"It was nice to meet *you,* Mrs. Parrot."

"Call me Zilla."

Mum wandered off.

"Actually her real name's Barbara," I told Poppy. "But don't call her that."

We met Zoran at a hat stall. He was there with Mrs. Zoran, who looked rather like him. Her expression was just as serious, her eyes just as dark. However, her hair was jet-black while Zoran's had weird brown and yellow streaks in it. Mr. and Mrs. Zoran were trying on home-made hats, brightly colored ones like court jesters used to wear. It was odd to see two serious people trying on such strange hats.

"Hello, Zoran."

"Hello Set."

"You should get Franca to fix your hair."

"I did."

"It looks very nice," I said.

"Zoran, put on this one." Mrs. Zoran handed her husband a purple hat, which he tried on.

"It suits you," gushed the hatmaker, who was round and plump. She was hardly going to tell Zoran that he looked like a big Slavic buffoon.

"In Serbia you would be stoned to death for wearing hat like this," said Zoran.

"Don't talk cacka," said Mrs. Zoran. "No one gets stoned to death in Serbia these days."

"Or pushed out of window by secret police." Zoran took off the purple hat.

Mrs. Zoran tried on a bright blue and green one with a bell.

"What you think?" she asked.

"Horrible," said Zoran.

"I will buy it." Mrs. Zoran took some money out of her purse.

"If you were accountant you would not dare to wear hat like that," said Zoran. "You would get no respect."

"But I am not accountant, thank God." Mrs. Zoran handed over her money to the grinning hatmaker.

Poppy appeared in a huge green and silver hat. "How do I look?"

"Worse than my wife," said Zoran. "You should buy it."

Poppy bought the green and silver hat, one that would get her stoned to death in Serbia.

Jack and India were lying on the grass in front of a stage area. They were both wearing the same outfits—bright blue Lycra shorts and crop tops. India was playing with a big fluffy bee on elastic that had been made in an overseas sweatshop. Jack had bought it for her. Poppy and I joined them, even though I was embarrassed about the Lycra and the bee.

"That's a good hat," Jack told Poppy. "You look like a model." He probably thought I was interested in Poppy, so he was trying to charm her away from me. India noticed this and played for Jack's attention.

"I love oo, Jack."

Eurgghh!

"I love you too, precious."

Then India and Jack smooched and made little pussycat noises. I looked away in disgust. If I ever kissed Miranda, it'd be a proper pash. We'd roll around like wild animals. It wouldn't be the ghastly little kisses that Jack and India were giving each other. Fortunately, the Phantom Pig tipped a bucket of silver confetti over them and they stopped.

"Jack, can I have a ice cream?" asked India, picking the silver stuff out of her hair.

"Of course you can, precious. Get me one too, please."

"I thought you were lactose intolerant," I said.

"I got better," said Jack.

I felt a stinging pain in my arm and looked down to see a bull-ant crawling off into the grass. I swore.

"Um-ah! Seth said a rude word!" said India.

"Don't say rude words in front of my fiancée," said Jack.

I showed them what had happened.

"Did oo get bitten by a ant?" India asked.

"Yes!" God she was annoying with her baby talk.

"Oo poor boy!"

"Shut up," I said.

"Don't tell my fiancée to shut up," Jack said.

"You shut up."

"Rude gestures!"

"Rude gestures to *you*!"

"Extremely rude gestures to you!"

"Enormously rude gestures to you!"

"That's enough rude gestures," Poppy said. "Come with me, Seth."

•

We went to six herbalists. They all seemed disturbed by the ant bite, which looked red and angry against my pale skin. One herbalist rubbed on some aloe vera. Another offered to sell me a wind chime. Finally, we went to the St. John Ambulance at the front gate. An officer looked at my arm, then sprayed it with something that made it hurt less. He told me that if the pain didn't go in an hour, I should come back and get some paracetamols. I'd have to sign a form saying I wasn't a drug addict.

I overheard an argument nearby and recognized the voices of Dad and Mr. Raven. Poppy and I hung back and listened. Dad was in a truly foul mood.

"It's not possible," he said.

"You'll need to get at least eight more," said Mr. Raven.

"Portable toilets are very hard to arrange at short notice."

"Then you didn't plan properly."

"We weren't expecting this many people."

"You should have foreseen this."

Dad could bear it no longer and launched into one of his tirades.

"Of course. I forgot that I have the ability to see into the future."

"Don't be absurd!"

"I'm looking into the future right now, Mr. Raven, and it's fascinating. There's been a bloody revolution, the town hall is burning and I'm afraid your head has been stuck on the end of a large pole. People are laughing and cheering and there's a huge celebration on the sports oval that will require exactly twenty-four Portaloos."

"You're wasting precious time."

Dad took a deep breath. "Why are you antagonizing me?"

"I'm just doing my job," said Mr. Raven, "and helping other people do theirs."

"You're doing it in a very officious way. You're singling me out."

"Mr. Parrot, be reasonable. Why would I do that? Now organize those extra Portaloos."

Dad sighed and made a phone call. I tried to creep away so Dad wouldn't know I'd witnessed the scene. But he saw Poppy and me while he was on the phone. Even though he was stressed, he beckoned us over. Dad took a credit card from his pocket and read out the number to the Portaloo hire company. Then he finished his call and smiled at Poppy and me as if everything were fine.

"Hello, Seth."

"Hi, Dad."

"You must be Miranda," Dad said to Poppy.

"No, Dad!" I said it far too loudly, as if this were too ridiculous for words.

"I'm in the drama class with Seth," Poppy said.

"Of course," said Dad. "Of course you are."

We left Dad to supervise the arrival of the Portaloos. Poppy didn't ask who Miranda was. But she'd guessed she was someone special to me. She looked a bit sad, not the sort of person who should be wearing a big green and silver hat. Poppy told me she was meeting some friends on the other side of the oval and she had to go. I was alone again.

I saw Mr. Raven in the car park, chatting with a parking officer. Something in me snapped. I walked over to Mr. Raven and, like an idiot, confronted him.

"Why are you picking on us?"

Mr. Raven was angry to be interrupted. "I'm not picking on anyone. I'm making sure that public health and safety standards are maintained."

"Do you have to be such a pain in the arse about it?"

I'd wanted to come across as forceful. I knew I'd just sounded pathetic.

"Kindly allow me to return to my conversation," said Mr. Raven. "You've been most discourteous. I see you're no better than your father."

I hung my head. There was nothing else I could say. And that was when I noticed the wallet. It was lying a short distance from Mr. Raven's spotless shoes, in the shade of a parked car. It was the neatest-looking wallet I'd ever seen. Surely it belonged to Mr. Raven. I pretended to wander off, and waited near the St. John Ambulance for Mr. Raven to finish his conversation with the parking officer. Would he walk away without realizing he was missing his wallet? How could I turn this to my advantage?

The two men went their separate ways. I returned to the car, which had a crisp new parking ticket stuck to the windscreen. I looked around, then bent down and pretended to tie my shoelaces. The wallet was still there. I grabbed it and shoved it in my pocket.

As I walked past the main gate, I saw a truck delivering the extra Portaloos. I memorized the phone number on the side of the truck. Now all I needed was a public telephone booth.

Kinglet's main street was deserted. Everyone was on the football oval having their auras read or being mimed at. All the phone booths outside the post office were empty. After three attempts, I found one that worked. Furtively, I opened the wallet to make sure it belonged to Mr. Raven. My heart sank when I saw the driver's license. The man in the photo was not Mr. Raven. He was a pleasant-looking man with dark hair. So much for my brilliant scheme! Then I realized that this was an old license, issued nearly ten years ago. Time hadn't been kind to Jeff Raven. The smiling man in the photo was him.

"Sani-boy Toilet Hire," said the woman at the other end of the line.

I tried to sound as official as possible.

"I represent the Currawong Council."

"How can we help you?" asked the woman.

"I'm just ringing to say how pleased we are with the service you've provided for our Earthlight Festival. You've been prompt and professional."

"I'll pass your comments on to our managing director."

"However, it seems we require more toilets."

"More toilets?"

"Yes."

"When would you need them?"

"Immediately." I heard the woman tap a computer.

"Are you aware ten portable toilets have just been dispatched to Kinglet Oval?" she asked.

"We're very happy with them," I said. "They're magnificent. We just need a few more."

"I'm afraid I can only offer you six at the moment." The woman told me how much the toilets would cost. I hesitated. Thinking up the scheme had been exciting, but now that I was about to go through with it, I felt guilty. It went against the Mr. Right list. Then I remembered how much I hated Mr. Raven for tormenting my father. He deserved everything he got. I read out Mr. Raven's credit card details over the phone.

"We'll have them to you within an hour," said the woman.

"That'd be most helpful," I said.

"Same address?"

I looked at Mr. Raven's driver's license.

"No, these toilets are for another function we're holding not far away. At a private house."

I read out Mr. Raven's address.

"Will there be someone there to advise where the toilets should be positioned?"

"Anywhere on the property will be fine," I said. "But ideally they should all be in the front garden."

•

It was nearly noon when I got back to the car park. I tossed the wallet back under the car. My first thought was to race off and tell Dad about my brilliant plan. Then I realized it'd be better to sit back and let the scene play itself out.

The festival was a success, even if Casper and Jasper burst the bouncy castle. The usual closing fireworks were confiscated for safety reasons. A local thrash metal band called Mind Control made up for it by playing a three-hour set, with the Phantom Pig dancing madly as the sun went down. The St. John Ambulance officers attended to twelve severe cases of sunburn because some people had decided to swim in the river without their bathers. One of them was Mr. Kenvyn.

FACT SEVEN

Penguins like bananas

When they finally got home from the festival, Mum and Dad were exhausted and snitchy. It was past two in the morning, but I hadn't fallen asleep yet. Three hundred sit-ups hadn't helped.

"I *told* you to organize more than last year," Mum said to Dad. They were trying not to make too much noise.

"I *did* organize more. Last year there were six. This year I organized ten. Ten is more than six."

"I meant a *lot* more."

"Then you should've *said* a lot more!" Dad caught himself. "I'm sorry, Zilla. I didn't mean to snap."

Mum sighed. "It shouldn't be so hard to order the right number of portable toilets. It isn't rocket science."

"I hate that expression," said Dad. "I wonder what they say at NASA if someone botches up? You couldn't say, 'It isn't rocket science,' because of course it actually would be."

"What are you talking about, Eric?"

"I don't know, I'm tired."

"We'll have to pay a lot more for those extra toilets. They make you pay a premium if you don't order them forty-eight hours in advance."

"Mr. Raven was very officious about it, too, the mean old git."

"Eric, I forbid you to mention that man again. I'm sick to death of hearing his name."

"But if you'd heard the way he spoke ..."

"That's enough! If you had a job like mine you'd know how to deal with people like Jeff Raven. It's called mediation. I might even start a course at the Center. You could learn a thing or two."

While Mum stomped to the bathroom to wash off her clown makeup, Dad picked up his guitar and played a few sad bars.

A piece of render fell off my bedroom wall.

The Phantom Pig ended up on the cover of the local paper for the third year in a row. The headline was: EARTHTIGHT FESTIVAL A 'PIG' SUCCESS! On the letters page was an apology from the editor, saying that the letter from Dr. William Shatner about Mr. Raven being a chromus domus was a forgery. The editor pointed out that William Shatner was not an anthropologist. He was an American actor who was famous for playing the role of Captain Kirk in the old TV show *Star Trek*. And Mr. Raven was not a chromus domus. He was the senior environmental health officer for the district of Currawong.

At breakfast, Jack made an announcement as we all ate our homemade muesli.

"I've found out I'm probably color-blind."

"How do you know you're color-blind?" Dad asked.

"Everything is too green," said Jack.

"How do you know it's too green?" I asked.

"India has a book with eye tests in it. And when we tested each other, we found out that we're both color-blind."

"Well, we'd better take you to Dr. Penhaligon," said Dad. "It's a shame, because I believe there are visa restrictions in South Africa. They don't let you into the country if you're color-blind."

"Are you sure about that?" asked Jack.

"Pretty sure. If you're color-blind you won't be able to see the animals properly, which means you might get too close. The local people don't like it when the tourists get eaten. It looks bad in the travel brochures."

Dad and I exchanged knowing looks over the muesli.

"We might've done the tests wrong," said Jack. "I don't think I should see Dr. Penhaligon just yet."

"Fair enough," said Dad. "But I'm concerned about that mark on your neck. It's not some kind of leprosy, is it?"

"It's a love bite. India did it."

"Ah, so it is," said Dad. "I used to give your mother love bites."

"No you didn't," said Mum. "I hate love bites."

"I seem to remember we bit each other all the way through *Alien,*" said Dad.

"I think you're confusing me with someone else," said Mum.

"You *are* my wife, aren't you? Zilla Parrot, Aquarian, drives a Toyota?"

"Yes, Eric, I am your wife."

Mum made it sound like a jail sentence, or at least community service.

Mr. Raven, his tie askew and his top button undone, arrived on our doorstep just as Dad was leaving for work.

"Mr. Raven, this is an unexpected pleasure," cried Dad. Jack, Mum and I quickly gathered around. "What brings you here?"

"Six portable toilets on my front lawn!" replied Mr. Raven, trembling.

Dad looked flabbergasted. "Six portable toilets?"

"I came home to see half a dozen portable lavatories in my garden! I live in a quiet suburban street, Mr. Parrot. People don't like it when armies of toilets suddenly appear!"

"I imagine they were horrified!" Dad bit his lip. He made sure to keep his toes out of range of Mum's stomping foot. "But I fail to see why you've come to visit. This awful toilet infestation has nothing to do with me."

"I've sent them back," said Mr. Raven. "They came from the hire company you contacted on Saturday. Wouldn't you say that's quite a coincidence?"

"Yes, I would," Dad admitted.

"Someone paid for them, quoting *my* credit card details. I have a cat, Mr. Parrot. The poor creature is traumatized. He's an old cat and doesn't react well to change. You can imagine Churchill's horror at seeing the garden full of cubicles!"

"And Churchill would be your cat?" said Dad.

Mum snapped. "Of course Churchill's his cat, Eric!"

"Don't jump to conclusions, Zilla. Mr. Raven might be referring to his wife."

And Mum did manage to stomp on Dad's toe.

"Credit card fraud is a serious crime," said Mr. Raven, "and you're as guilty as hell!"

"Please temper your language, Mr. Raven. The shock has unbalanced you."

"I intend to take this matter to the police."

"Well, I certainly hope they locate the culprit. Six Portaloos in your front garden, you say? Dreadful. Perfectly dreadful."

"Good day, Mr. Parrot."

"Good day, Mr. Raven."

Dad closed the front door and collapsed with laughter. So did Jack. I'd been so proud of my clever stunt, but now it gave me a queasy feeling.

"Eric, have you gone stark staring raving bonkers?" Mum yelled.

"I didn't do it, Zilla. Cross my heart and hope to die. Someone else must hate the mean old coot as much as I do."

I decided to keep quiet about what I'd done. I was now a criminal guilty of credit card fraud.

In drama class we had a workshop of "Night of Fear." Everyone acted out scenes, then suggested how my play could be improved. Tyrone said it needed songs. Casper and Jasper said it needed fights. Jack and India said it needed kissing. Lukas said nothing. Poppy said all the characters sounded the same and I should give them different voices. Will Stretton said Poppy's was the strongest idea. Then Poppy said the play also needed some poems. Will Stretton said her first idea was better.

In the kitchenette, Miranda was wearing green harem pants and a camouflage tank top. She looked like she'd just completed a set of push-ups, and her biceps bulged. There was no one else in the kitchenette. Was Miranda actually waiting there for me?

"Hi," said Miranda.

"Hi," I said.

"Your haircut looks better."

I appreciated the compliment but didn't want to seem vain, because the Mr. Right list said I shouldn't be. "I'm not sure about the veranda bit," I said.

"I like the veranda."

"Thank you, Miranda."

We were sounding like Dr. Seuss.

"How was the drama class?"

I told Miranda we'd done a workshop of "Night of Fear." She seemed impressed that I'd written a play, but I remained modest.

"What's your play about?"

"Death," I said, modestly.

"So I guess it's not a comedy?"

"No, it's a very serious play."

"I thought you'd write funny plays."

"Why?"

"Well, some of your comments are sort of … funny," said Miranda. "That's a compliment," she added.

Counting the compliment she'd made about my haircut, that made two in three minutes. I should probably compliment Miranda to make things even.

"I like your top," I said.

"Thanks."

"And I like the way you sweat."

Miranda chuckled. "That's the kind of comment I mean."

I pretended it was meant to be a joke. But I honestly did like the way Miranda sweated. There was an old expression Dad taught me: horses sweat, men perspire, women glow. But I didn't want a glowing woman. That would have been eerie.

"What did you think of the wheatgrass juice?" I asked.

"I couldn't try it. We don't have the right type of juicer."

"What a shame!" I said.

"Yes."

"Have you still got the wheatgrass?"

Miranda nodded. "I kept it in the fridge. Dad wanted to throw it out, but I said it was a science experiment."

"I could lend you a juicer," I said. "When can I drop it around? What about tomorrow afternoon? Would that be too soon? I could make it later if you'd prefer. Only I'll be free tomorrow afternoon and we shouldn't leave it for too long, because the wheatgrass is probably on its last legs. Not that wheatgrass has legs."

"Tomorrow would be good," said Miranda.

We made a time, and exchanged addresses and phone numbers.

"I just realized, I don't even know your last name," I said.

"It's Raven."

I felt like I'd been punched in the abdominals and had to sit down.

"Is your dad Jeff Raven?" I asked.

"Yes."

"The environmental health officer?"

"That's him."

"Are you sure?"

"What's the problem?"

"No problem. I just didn't realize your father was so ... famous."

"I don't know your last name either," Miranda said.

Had Mr. Raven told Miranda about the dreadful family in Jacana Avenue? Parrot was a fairly unusual name. If Mr. Raven had mentioned it, Miranda would have remembered.

"It's Banerjee," I stammered. "My last name is Banerjee."

"Isn't that an Indian name?"

"Yes, my father comes from India."

"Which part?"

"All of him."

"You don't look very Indian. Your hair's too red."

"I'm a red Indian."

Miranda chuckled again.

What could I do? More than anything, I wanted to be with Miranda, to make wheatgrass juice for her. But I couldn't go to her house after what I'd said to her father. And I couldn't bring Miranda to my house because Jack would seduce her.

Miranda was rehydrating again.

"I don't think this is going to work out," I said.

"What do you mean? Why not?"

"Well, I'm not sure your dad would approve."

"I can have boys around."

I felt jealous and wondered how many boys had come around to Miranda's house. Six? Ten? A hundred?

"I don't have a boyfriend at the moment," said Miranda, reading my face. "Anyway, you don't have to worry because Dad's working late tomorrow."

"What about your mum?"

"I don't have a mum."

"Great!"

"What?"

"I mean it's not great that you don't have a mum. But it's great that you're free tomorrow afternoon and that your father will be at work and that I'll be able to come over and lend you a juicer."

"Are you *sure* you've written a serious play?" asked Miranda.

"Very serious," I said. "Very, very serious."

Should I tell Dad that the girl I liked in the kickboxing class was actually Mr. Raven's daughter? Should I tell him that I had sent the Portaloos to Mr. Raven's house? I decided to ask Zoran for advice. I was obviously desperate.

As I filled Zoran in on the Miranda situation, he picked up snails from the garden and dropped them in a bucket.

"We have an expression in Serbia," said Zoran. "You are in deep cacka."

"We have a similar expression here," I said.

"Is she beautiful, this girl?"

"She is the most beautiful creature in the whole world."

"And her father is horrible ugly bald man?"

"Yes."

"Then maybe this girl will grow up to be horrible ugly bald woman. Look on bright side. Maybe you better without her."

"You don't understand. I *need* to be with her. With every fiber of my being I ache for her. I'm in love!"

"I do understand. It was same for me with Mrs. Zoran when I first meet her. But the feeling goes away after few hours."

"Could I pick some flowers for Miranda?" I asked.

"You cannot take these flowers," said Zoran. "They belong to the government."

"You're beginning to like them, aren't you?"

"I hate these flowers. They torment me with their ugly colors and their sickly smells. I hate them all."

Kids had been digging up worms for fishing in the river. Zoran cursed as he found the evidence of their excavation.

"These kids is criminals. In Serbia they would have bricks tied to their legs and be dropped in sea."

"Just for taking worms?"

"*Government* worms."

"Well, *you're* taking all the snails."

"Snails is pests. But flowers need worms to aerate the soil."

Aerate didn't seem the sort of word a Serbian flower hater should know.

"What are you going to do with the snails?" I asked.

"Eat them."

"Really?"

"Of course not, stupid boy. This is Australia. I don't have to eat snails. I can eat Australian food like pizza. Only in Serbia do people have to eat snails. If they can't find snails, they eat wood."

"So what are you *really* going to do with the snails?"

"Kill them."

This brought out the yin in me.

"Do you have to?" I asked.

"You want eat them?"

"No."

"You want give them to your girlfriend as present?"

"No."

"Then I kill them. You see? At least you should be glad you are not snail."

At home I helped Mum pack up some books to give to the Brotherhood shop. They were mainly about subjects like hydroponics and tie-dye. One of the books was about sex education.

"You might like to look at that one, Seth," said Mum.

"It looks old."

"Sex doesn't go out of date. Not like tie-dye."

The question had been building up in me for so long that I just blurted it out. "Mum, do you think you and Dad will ever do it again?"

Mum gave the question careful consideration. "No," she said finally.

"Why not?"

"It was expensive and it ruined our clothes."

"Sex?"

"I thought you were talking about tie-dye."

"I meant sex. Between you and Dad."

Mum put the sex book in the pile for the Brotherhood, a charity started by monks.

"Seth, it's not appropriate to discuss this. It's a matter for Eric and me."

"You're always saying how important it is to talk."

"Some things are better left unsaid."

We finished packing the books. Mum was feeling guilty about being uncommunicative. Now would be a good time to ask her for a favor.

"Mum, could I borrow something of yours, please?"

"Depends what it is."

"Your juicer. Could I please borrow your juicer?"

"Of course you can."

"The thing is, I'll need to take it somewhere."

"You mean, like on a holiday?"

"This is serious, Mum."

"Where do you want to take it?"

"I can't really tell you."

"Why not?"

"Because some things are better left unsaid."

Mum actually chuckled, so there was hope. I just wished she'd start laughing with Dad again.

After school the next day, I pedaled my bike along the river all the way from Kinglet to Gang Gang. I was wearing new board shorts and a Mambo shirt with a dog on it. It was the best shirt I owned and I'd bought it at a warehouse sale. Jack told me it looked like the dog on the shirt was farting. I told him he was childish.

Miranda's house was unlike ours in every way. There was a neat front garden, a picket fence and a rather ordinary letterbox, nothing like Dad's magnificent creation. The lawn was very short. If you looked closely (which of course I did) you could see six square impressions where portable toilets had recently stood. This was Mr. Raven's lair. I prayed Miranda was right and that he wasn't home.

Miranda answered the door, dressed in combat pants

and a white tank top. She looked a bit like Linda Hamilton after doing all those chin-ups in *Terminator 2*.

"Hi, Seth."

"Are you alone?" I asked.

"Apart from Churchill."

"I brought the juicer." I held it out in front of me.

Miranda smiled. "Then you'd better come in."

"Thanks."

"I like your shirt."

"Thanks."

"It's got a farting dog on it."

I laughed.

Inside Miranda's house were countless pictures of aircraft, hung in neat little rows on the wall. There were Starfighters, Spitfires, Messerschmitts, Hurricanes, Stukas, Hornets and Heinkels. There was even a Tornado in the toilet.

I set up the juicer on the island bench. A huge fluffy cat padded up to me and started rubbing against my legs. I scratched him under the chin.

"That's Churchill," said Miranda. "He's not fully recovered."

"Recovered from what?" I whisked my hand away, worried that Churchill might have ringworm.

"Someone sent six Portaloos to our house," said Miranda. "Churchill went catatonic."

"Well, he's a cat, so that makes sense."

"It's not funny."

"No, sorry. God, what a terrible thing to happen," I said. "Why would anyone send you six Portaloos?"

Miranda shrugged. "I guess there are some real psychos out there."

I washed the fur off my hands. The guilt remained.

Miranda produced the wilted wheatgrass from the back of the fridge. I turned the juicer on and it made a furious noise. Churchill ran screeching from the room. Those Portaloos had really freaked him out.

I cut off clumps of the wheatgrass and fed them into the juicer. Green liquid started to trickle out of the spout and into a glass. I passed the glass to Miranda and her hand touched mine. Miranda drank.

"What do you think?"

"It's like drinking a lawn," said Miranda, screwing up her nose. "Are you sure you're supposed to drink this stuff?"

I tried the juice. It was revolting.

"I think Mum mixes it with apple," I said.

Miranda found some apples and we fed them into the juicer. The combination tasted much better. Not too sweet, not too sour. Sort of yin/yang. Miranda brushed past me and I caught the whiff of Dencorub. Alarmed, I realized that I was experiencing a disturbance in the trousers. (This is what Jack and I called it. We knew the correct term but preferred "a disturbance in the trousers.") I immediately tried hard to think of the Chinese communist leader Chairman Mao, which usually helps in situations like this.

"I like all the pictures of the planes," I said. Chairman Mao Chairman Mao Chairman Mao.

"My dad is a little obsessed."

"Does your dad fly?" I asked. "I mean in a plane, of course. Not on his own. I mean, is he a pilot? When he's not being an environmental health officer?"

"No," said Miranda. "He's just an environmental health officer."

"What about your mother?"

"She's not a pilot either."

"What does she do?"

"She's dead."

"Oh God, I'm sorry. It's just, when you said you didn't have a mother, I thought ..."

"What did you think?"

"Well, half the kids in Kinglet have so many different assortments of parents you can never tell. I'm really sorry."

"That's okay, it was a while ago."

"That'd be the worst."

"It was a terrible time."

I rinsed and wiped the glass thoroughly, in case Mr. Raven later dusted it for fingerprints. Miranda put the glass away. What fantastic shoulders she had! Chairman Mao Great Wall Tiananmen Square.

"Would you like to go for a swim?" suggested Miranda.

"I didn't bring my Beijing costume."

"Did you say Beijing costume?"

"Yes. I meant to say bathing costume." Bloody Chairman Mao.

"Can't you swim in your underpants?"

"They're horrible and navy blue."

"Would you like to wear my harem pants?"

"Miranda, are you absolutely sure your father won't come home?"

"Not for hours. He's at a council meeting. Why are you so worried?"

"I'm not. And I'd really like to wear your harem pants."

Miranda's backyard was private, not exposed like ours. The bellbirds were too hot to make anything but the weakest attempt at a *ping*. Miranda was already in the pool. She was wearing a yellow one-piece. Her hair looked amazing when it was wet.

I lowered myself into the pool. The harem pants filled with air and made me look like I was wearing a barrage balloon on each leg.

"You have the reddest hair I've ever seen," said Miranda.

It wasn't quite a compliment, just a statement of fact, but I liked it.

"My gran calls me Carrot," I said. "Short for Carrot-top. Even though the tops of carrots are green, not red."

"I think Carrot's a good name."

"It doesn't go well with my surname. It rhymes."

Miranda looked puzzled. "Carrot doesn't rhyme with Banerjee."

I'd forgotten I'd lied about my name. "Miranda, have you ever heard of the name Parrot?"

"Is that a real name?"

I nodded. "It's my name."

"Why did you tell me it was Banerjee?"

"Well, Parrot sounds odd. I was embarrassed."

"Don't be embarrassed."

"Thanks."

"Though it is an odd name."

"Yes."

"My ex-boyfriend's name is George Jupitus," said Miranda.

"That's a bad name," I said. "He sounds like he should be wearing a cape and leaping over tall buildings."

"You wouldn't say that if you met him."

"Yes, I would."

"He's pretty big."

"But I'm wiry." I was also jealous.

"He plays football with the Gang Gang Under Sixteens. He was the best and fairest last year."

I could picture George Jupitus. A superhero with muscles on his muscles.

"We broke up ages ago," said Miranda. "He was a bit of a psycho."

I cheered up immensely. "What a shame. In what way was he a psycho exactly?"

"He was incredibly jealous."

"Jealousy is bad. I never get jealous."

"He hated boys who even looked at me."

Since most boys would look at Miranda, George had a lot of people to hate.

"He keeps ringing to say we should get back together," said Miranda.

"Don't!" I said desperately. "He isn't right for you. Find someone new."

"I decided to drop him after he bashed someone up and chucked them in the river."

I gasped. "*What?*"

"They didn't drown," said Miranda.

A gumleaf fluttered into the water. Miranda swam like a frog along the bottom of the pool. It didn't seem possible that a girl like Miranda could be my serious girlfriend. And yet, she didn't mind my daggy comments. She never rolled her eyes. And every now and then she glanced at my pectoralis major, which admittedly was in good shape. Miranda bobbed up and gently smoothed back her hair.

"What are you thinking about?" she asked.

"You could be a model," I said.

It was a boring thing to say. Unimaginative boys always said it to girls they liked. Jack got away with it because he was charismatic. But it was not the sort of thing Mr. Right would say. I tried to recall the list, but couldn't. Normally I could recite it from memory. Being with Miranda made me stupid. I attempted to be more inventive with my compliments.

"You look like Venus," I said. "The beautiful woman. Not the gassy planet."

"Are you really interested in kickboxing?" asked Miranda.

"Very."

"Let's try some jumpkicks."

We leaped higher and higher, aiming our feet at a sack of cotton waste that Miranda had hung from a ghost gum in the backyard. The sight of Miranda in her yellow swimsuit flying through the air and kicking did incredible things to me.

Then Miranda's dad came home.

Mr. Raven didn't look at all happy to find me kicking around in his daughter's harem pants.

"Dad, this is Seth," said Miranda.

Mr. Raven gave me a hideous look and walked into the house.

"Bugger!" I said.

FACT EIGHT

Peanuts are used in the production of dynamite

I changed into my Mambo clothes in the laundry, then crept out into the lounge room, where the pictures of airplanes hung in formation. Mr. Raven had changed into casual clothes that made him look less strict, but not much. Even his casual clothes looked like a uniform.

"You're home early," said Miranda, a little nervously.

Mr. Raven grunted.

"Seth came over to lend me a juicer."

"I wondered what that thing was," muttered Mr. Raven.

"I like your pictures of planes," I said, probably sounding insane. "Especially the Lockheed Starfighter."

"That's a Douglas Dakota."

Mr. Raven didn't look at me, as if the sight of me caused him physical pain.

"Seth made me a juice drink," said Miranda.

"Fascinating."

"Do you want to try it?"

"I'd prefer to drink paint."

Churchill leaped into Mr. Raven's lap and made himself comfortable. I couldn't believe any creature in the world could find Mr. Raven comfortable to sit on.

"You have a picture of the Wright brothers' plane," I said.

Mr. Raven grunted again.

"I admire the Wright brothers," I said, desperately trying to make him like me. "Did you see how they tried to re-enact their first flight?" This was one of the facts that Dad had told me, and I thought even Mr. Raven might find it interesting. "Some pilots went back to the place where the Wright brothers flew their plane and tried to fly a replica. They got beaten about so badly by all the falls that they could only do a few flights each. But Wilbur and Orville Wright had done it over and over again. They were so convinced their plane would fly, they just kept going back day after day, knocking themselves about but never giving up. You *have* to admire that."

I'd given a superb performance. Mr. Raven would surely look at me in a whole new light.

"Please shut up," said Mr. Raven.

"I'm really sorry about what happened," I said.

"I have great difficulty believing someone in a shirt with a flatulent dog on it."

"I should go," I said to Miranda.

"What's going on?" Miranda asked. Mr. Raven had obviously kept his Parrot battles a secret from his daughter, just as she'd kept her visits to the SLC a secret from him. It seemed they had communication difficulties.

"I personally feel very bad about this whole business," I said. "I wish it hadn't got to this stage."

"I personally feel you should go before I throw that juicer at your head," said Mr. Raven.

•

Carrying Mum's juicer, I walked with Miranda down to her front gate. I felt numb.

"What was all that about?"

"You'll find out," I said.

"Well, thanks for bringing the juicer."

"Miranda, come inside!" Mr. Raven yelled from the front door.

"Good-bye, Carrot," said Miranda.

"Miranda, I forbid you to have anything to do with that boy!"

"Yes, Dad."

"I'm serious! If I ever find you consorting with him I'll punish you severely."

What would he do? Fine her? Jail her? Dunk her in Kinglet River like a witch?

"Yes, Dad."

Miranda went back inside.

"Young man, you're never to visit this house again!" called Mr. Raven.

I miserably rode back home along the river, carrying Mum's juicer. I'd been riding for a few minutes when I realized there was a cyclist following me. He was a huge creature in football shorts and a Gang Gang Under Sixteens training singlet. I was about to encounter George Jupitus, the psycho with the superhero name.

I knew I couldn't outride him, so I climbed off my bike and waited for him to skid to a halt. I wasn't scared, I told myself. I'd be able to stand up to a jealous ex-boyfriend, even one like George Jupitus. I'd reason with him, man to man. Well, man to monolith.

"Who are you?" George spoke quietly, like Hannibal Lecter just before he eats someone's liver.

"I'm Seth. You must be George."

"Did Miranda tell you about me?"

"Yes."

"What did she say?"

How should I play this?

"Not much," I said.

George sized me up. I sized him up. He was taller than I was, and his arms looked bigger than my legs. "So what are you up to?" he asked.

"I'm just riding home."

"I mean with Miranda."

"Nothing. Her father doesn't like me, so I probably won't be seeing her again."

"What's that?" George pointed at the juicer.

I explained what it was for. I didn't go into detail about wheatgrass or the Aztecs.

"I was watching you," said George. "When you were jumping and doing those kicks. What was all that about?"

Oh God, the guy was a stalker.

"We were just mucking around," I said.

"I don't want you mucking around with Miranda."

George punched me in the stomach. It hurt like hell and I fell to the ground.

"Do you understand me?" said George.

I was winded, so I just nodded.

"Do you understand me?"

"Yes," I gasped.

George picked up Mum's juicer, examined it for a moment and tossed it into the river. Then he climbed on his bike and rode off. If George Jupitus was the best and fairest of the Gang Gang Under Sixteens, the rest of the team must have been axe murderers.

After ten minutes I felt okay again. There was a massive bruise on my stomach. (We redheads are terrible bruisers.) I waded into the river to see if I could retrieve Mum's juicer. But George was a good thrower. He'd managed to land the juicer in the middle of the torrent, where the water was deepest. A police skin-diving team might have been able to salvage it, but I certainly couldn't.

I didn't break the news to Mum immediately. She loved her juicer. Its drowning would come as a bitter blow. And I didn't tell anyone about George Jupitus. Not for the moment.

That night at dinner we tucked into the pakoras with raita and chickpeas that Dad had made.

"You seem quiet, Seth," said Dad.

"Just thinking about my play," I lied.

"How's the rewriting coming along?" asked Mum.

"Really well."

I hadn't rewritten a thing. My life was becoming too complicated to do another draft of a play that was already perfect. Jack was concerned about not being the center of attention for a few seconds.

"I've decided to get dreadnoughts," said Jack.

Mum looked up. "Dreadnoughts?"

"A lot of the natives in Africa have dreadnoughts in their hair. So I thought I'd do it, too."

"Dreadlocks," said Dad. "Not dreadnoughts."

"Dreadnoughts are battleships," I said. "You'd look pretty stupid with battleships in your hair."

"India's going to get them, too."

"How are things with India?" Dad asked.

"We're still going to get married. And we intend to have children. We're practicing all the time."

Dad and Mum both choked on their pakoras.

"*What?*"

"We're practicing what it'll be like to be responsible for a child," said Jack. "We've been using Mr. Banerjee as a child-substitute. We took him to the park today. Next we'll take him to the pictures."

"Mr. Banerjee is quite large," Mum said.

"We figure he's about the same size as a two-year-old human."

"I'm not sure they'll let you take such a large toy into the pictures," said Mum.

"We'll buy him an extra seat. We're taking our responsibility as parents very seriously."

There was a fine line between being individual and being bonkers, and I thought Jack had crossed it.

•

Throughout recorded history, there had been no pre-emptive missile strikes in Jacana Avenue. So we were all surprised by the first explosion. We were even more surprised by the following ten, especially as they were happening right outside our house. Vivid pink light flooded through the windows.

Mum, Dad, Jack and I dashed out into the front garden, which now smelled heavily of gunpowder. The air was hot. The flashes were so bright that they hurt the eyes. The colors were ridiculously pretty for weapons of mass destruction. We stared in wonder as the explosions kept coming, and hissing balls of light went soaring into the air, where they erupted into huge dandelions. Mr. Robbins came out of his house to look. Two feral kids (Freebie and Zizmo) dressed in nothing but their undies and ugg boots, cried out "Ooh!" and "Ahh!" as each new incendiary spun and popped and dazzled.

This was a fireworks display and not a pre-emptive strike after all. But as the spectacle subsided and the gray smoke cleared, we saw what terrible damage had been done. Where Dad's letterbox had once stood, there was now a blackened post with nothing but some splinters of wood dangling. We waited for a few minutes in case there were more explosions, but it seemed all the fireworks were spent. Dad told us to stay back. He fetched the bucket of gray water from the kitchen, then approached the smoking ruin at our front gate. He tossed the water over what remained of the letterbox. It hissed angrily. The show was over. Freebie and Zizmo wandered back home.

"What a tragedy!" said Mr. Robbins, who knew how proud Dad was of his letterbox. "What do you think happened, exactly?"

"I'd say someone posted a bunch of firecrackers through the slot, then set light to them," said Dad.

"But who on earth would do such a terrible thing?"

"I don't know," said Dad.

A psychopath, I decided, was the most likely culprit.

FACT NINE

An elephant can sniff water from five kilometers away

"Seth, where is my juicer?"

Mum was craving her morning fix of wheatgrass juice, but she couldn't find her state-of-the-art German juice extractor. There was no point in lying.

"I'm afraid there was a freak accident," I said.

"What type of freak accident?"

"Your juicer is at the bottom of Kinglet River."

"What on earth is it doing there?"

"Mum, I tried to rescue it. But the current is too strong and the water is too deep."

"You still haven't told me how my juicer ended up on the bottom of Kinglet River. Surely it didn't commit suicide?"

I swallowed. "This maniac attacked me. He punched me in the guts and then he chucked your juicer away."

Mum didn't seem to believe the story. But when I held up my shirt to reveal the huge blue bruise over my abs, she was horrified.

"We should notify the police," said Mum.

"I'd prefer you didn't," I said.

"But you've been badly hurt."

"Not really."

"Do you know anything about your attacker?"

"Only that he's right-handed and extremely strong."

"What is *wrong* with the world?" It was too much for Mum. She rang work and said she'd be in late. Karen, Mum's assistant, told her not to worry. She'd take charge and everything would be fine. Since Karen was frightened of the photocopier, this wasn't likely. Karen couldn't run a bath, let alone the SLC.

I found Dad moping in the front garden, unable to summon up the energy to go to work.

"You'd better ring the office," I told Dad.

"Yes," he said.

"Give me your phone, Dad."

He took the phone from his pocket and handed it over. I pressed speed-dial and got through to Dad's boss. I reported that Eric Parrot would be unable to come to work today as there'd been a tragedy in the family. When the boss asked what the tragedy was, I mentioned the exploding letterbox.

The boss was surprisingly unsympathetic.

"Cheer up, Dad." I handed the phone back. Deep down I was feeling terrible. I was sure George was the firework-bomber. This meant I was partly responsible. And I still hadn't owned up about using Jeff Raven's credit card to pay for the Portaloos. A huge cloud of guilt, much thicker than last night's gunpowder smoke, surrounded me. But I reminded Dad of his hero's advice. "'There's nothing better for being sad than to learn something.'"

I suggested more kickboxing practice. Dad wandered off disconsolately to the shed to find his kickboxing pad, then we spent some time in the backyard together, leaping and yelling. This seemed to lift Dad's spirits.

I'd been attacked by a psycho and threatened by Mr. Raven, yet I still loved Miranda. I had a remarkable dream where Miranda and I were both on top of a ziggurat in Mexico, about to be sacrificed by a masked Aztec priest with a massive knife. We'd been stripped down to our undies. Even though we were stressed and about to die, I couldn't help noticing that Miranda wore fetching hipster knickers and a camouflage bra. I looked down at my own hideous blue briefs. At least it was good to see that I was developing a six-pack from all the sit-ups. The priest raised his blade high and it glinted in the sun. At the last moment, he was pushed aside by a group of six people in white coats. They kicked the priest off the top of the ziggurat, and he fell screaming to an ugly death.

"Are you all right?" asked the people in the white coats.

I nodded, as they untied the bonds.

"We're the *Dolly* psychologists," they explained. "We're here to remind you of rule twenty-one on the Mr. Right list. This dream has been a community service announcement."

In the next drama class, Tyrone handed out cards that had photos of surf lifesavers with their Speedos pulled up their cracks. Nangret said that the photos were an invasion of privacy because the surf lifesavers wouldn't know they'd been photographed. I figured that if the surf lifesavers wanted to patrol the beaches with their Speedos pulled up their cracks, they had it coming. The cards were party invitations. Tyrone was turning twenty-one on the weekend and we were all invited to a pool party at his house. It would be a good party. Gay people know how to throw a good party. Tyrone had a handsome older boyfriend called Kieran. They lived in one of the best houses in Kinglet. Some vandal once painted graffiti on their fence: POFS LIVE HERE. (The vandal might have worked for the local paper.)

Poppy read out her new poem before the class started because she was afraid there mightn't be time at the end.

"Love is painful, love is tough
Sometimes it can make you feel really rough
Love is something that happens to you
Just when you least expect it to.
You could be going for a walk,
Or listening to quite an interesting talk,
When all of a sudden you feel a pain,
O no! You've fallen in love again!
I wish that I was not in love,
I'd much prefer a little pet dove,
Or even a lovely emu chick,
But I'm in love and it makes me sick!"

Jack and India had brought Mr. Banerjee, their two-year-old

child, to the class. Casper and Jasper had a cigarette lighter and burned part of Mr. Banerjee's trunk. The smell of scorched synthetic material was toxic and we had to leave the room for a while. India sniffed and Jack angrily told the twins that they should be sent to a juvenile detention center for attempting to melt a child.

When the fumes cleared we returned to the drama room. Will Stretton announced that he'd cast "Night of Fear." I should have been excited, but I wasn't. Just a few rooms away, Miranda was doing jumpkicks. If she were thinking of me, they probably weren't good thoughts. Not after what her father would have told her.

Everyone got a part in the play, except for the twins.

"Why aren't we in it?" demanded Casper and Jasper.

"You aren't strong enough actors," said Will Stretton.

Casper and Jasper said they were extremely strong and put each other in headlocks to prove it.

"I've another role for you boys," said Will, after they'd calmed down. "Putting on a good play is a team effort. The actors onstage are only part of that team. Others work behind the scenes. For example, there are people who do makeup."

"We don't want to do makeup," said Casper and Jasper.

"Others do costumes and lighting," said Will.

"We don't want to do costumes and lighting," said Casper and Jasper.

"But the most important people are the stage managers."

"What do they do?"

"They make sure the play runs smoothly. They run around with props and bits of staging. It's a tremendously difficult task. Now that I think about it, you may not have the skill for it."

"You're using reverse psychology," said Casper and Jasper.

"Yes, I am," said Will, realizing the twins were smarter than any of us thought. "But if you want to be involved in this production, that's what you'll do."

Casper and Jasper accepted the offer.

"I have only 13 lines," Nangret complained.

"They're very good lines," I said.

"But 13 is unlucky. And Tyrone has nearly a hundred lines."

"A true actor doesn't care how many lines he has," said Tyrone, "although in fact I have 113."

"Lukas has 28 lines and he can't even talk," complained Nangret.

"I can talk when there are things to say," said Lukas. (This is his only line in the whole book.)

"I'm happy with my part," said Poppy. "Even if it's not quite as big as Tyrone's."

"India and I are very happy with our parts," said Jack.

India gave a little girlie giggle.

"Everything will change," Will said. "Seth is doing another draft. How's it going, Seth?"

"Extremely well," I said.

"How much have you written?"

"Nothing."

"You're letting the team down."

"I've been busy."

"Can I help you in any way?"

I said no. Unless Will could dispose of Mr. Raven and George Jupitus, then get Miranda to fall hopelessly in love with me, he could be of no help to me at all.

Will told us there was a production of a play called *The Elephant Man*, to be staged at the SLC on the weekend by a company whose theater had burned down during a bushfire. It was about a man with a grotesquely deformed head. Will recommended that we all see the play. "It might even help you write your next draft of 'Night of Fear,' Seth," he added.

We spent the rest of the class doing yoga postures, which actors do. Actors seem to spend a lot of time doing anything but acting.

Bend the knees and bring the feet as close to the buttocks as possible with the soles of the feet flat on the floor.

Bend the arms at the elbows and place the palms of the hands flat on the floor under each shoulder with the fingers pointing toward the back, then thrust the body upwards.

Do not think of Miranda in her yellow swimsuit.

This is how you do The Wheel, a famous yoga posture. It helps you to enter a state of relaxation and well-being. It's agony if you don't obey the last instruction.

Something weird happened to the base of my spine. I didn't cry out with pain. That wouldn't have been manly. I excused myself from the drama class, wandered off to the kitchenette where the paracetamols were and closed the door. *Then* I cried out.

I sat miserably in the kitchenette, waiting for the paracetamols to work. I thought about the fun times Miranda and I had enjoyed here, times we'd probably never have again. There was the glass Miranda had used. There was the tea towel with the picture of Scotland. There was the container of rat bait on the floor beside the fridge.

I bent over and touched my toes several times, trying to undo the damage I'd done to my back. As I did my tenth spine roll, I became aware of a Dencorub smell. I looked between my legs. There was Miranda upside down, smiling at me. She looked sweatier and more alluring than ever in army disposal combats. Even upside down she was irresistible. Being bent double with your backside facing someone isn't the most flattering pose in the world. I snapped back upright, far too quickly. God it hurt.

"Are you in pain?" Miranda asked.

"Not at all," I said.

"I knew I'd find you here."

The classes were only half over. I asked Miranda how she knew.

"I heard you scream," said Miranda. "I was worried."

Miranda was *worried* about me?

"There was a freak yoga accident," I said. "I seem to have injured my lumbar region. But I'm all right."

"Oh."

"Could you stay for a few moments, in case there are complications?"

Miranda agreed to stay for a few moments.

"I'm sorry about my father," said Miranda. "He's not always like that."

"I'm sure he must be a good person deep down to have a daughter like you," I said, trying to be charming.

"I take after my mother," said Miranda.

"So do I. *My* mother, not your mother." The paracetamols were making me more stupid than usual.

"He's been through a rough time," said Miranda.

"I can tell."

"How can you tell?"

"Well, he's so … bald."

"You're weird sometimes, Carrot."

"At least I'm not a psycho like your ex-boyfriend," I said. "I met him."

"You did?"

"When I was riding home from your place."

Miranda frowned. "What did he do?"

"He threw Mum's juicer in the river. I think he also blew up our letterbox."

"Seriously?"

"Well, somebody did."

"I hate George!" said Miranda.

"I'm not crazy about him myself."

"I'll speak with him."

"Please don't. I can take care of myself."

"If you say so."

I didn't want Miranda to go, but it looked like she was about to. "Have you ever heard of Thai massage?" I asked.

"No," said Miranda.

"You have to walk on a person's back," I said. "Could you do it for me? I think it might help."

Not only were the paracetamols making me stupid, they were also making me bold. I'd never asked a girl to walk on my back before. Amazingly, Miranda agreed to do it.

We wandered into one of the "learning rooms" that wasn't being used. There was a pile of old mats in the corner. I lay on my stomach on one of the mats.

"Tell me if it hurts," said Miranda, nervously stepping onto my back in bare feet.

It didn't hurt at all. It felt intensely exciting.

"You're very good at this," I said. "You could walk on people for a living."

"My dad wants me to be a judge."

"You could do both. Be a judge during the day and walk on people at night."

Miranda continued to walk up and down my spine.

"What are you doing on the weekend?" Miranda asked. This wasn't a question I'd been expecting.

"I'm not sure," I said. "I'm meant to be rewriting my play. What about you?"

"No plans," said Miranda. "How do you feel now?"

"Like a footpath."

Miranda chuckled. I could have sworn she was flirting with me, though it was hard to tell without eye contact, and you can't have eye contact with someone who's walking up and down your back.

"Do you want to get together?" Miranda asked.

She *was* flirting with me!

"Miranda, I was under the impression your father would prefer we didn't see each other."

"I can get around him."

"By not telling him? Like you don't tell him about the kickboxing classes?"

"If you're not interested ..."

"I'm sorry. *Of course* I want to get together."

There was a poster for *The Elephant Man* on the wall. It had been done on a computer by someone who wasn't good with computers.

"Would you like to see a play?" I suggested.

"What sort of play?"

"It's called *The Elephant Man.* It's about someone with a seriously deformed head."

"That sounds interesting. When's it on?"

"Saturday night."

"Let's see it."

I'd have jumped for joy if I weren't lying down with a girl on my back.

FACT TEN

One of these facts is untrue

There was a photo of the cast of *The Elephant Man* in the local paper. None of them had deformed heads, so they obviously weren't in their stage makeup. They were all pointing at the poster advertising their play. The photographer at the local paper always thought it was important for his subjects to be pointing at something. I wondered if the photographer's own family album was full of relatives pointing at things.

On page 2 there was a story about an eight-year-old boy who'd fallen down an abandoned mineshaft while taking his dog for a walk in the foothills. The boy's dog had rushed to get help. A police officer (32) praised the dog and said that if it hadn't run to get help, the boy would probably have died. Police advised readers that anyone walking through the foothills should avoid falling down mines.

Miranda rang to say she'd meet me at the SLC at seven thirty, to see *The Elephant Man*. She'd lied to her father and said she was going to see the play with a girlfriend called Tamsin.

•

My back was still hurting, despite Miranda's Thai massage. I went to see Dr. Penhaligon and told him what had happened. He gave me some anti-inflammatories and warned that I shouldn't do yoga or let girls walk on me for at least a month.

Even though it was Saturday, Mum went to the Center to try to fix the damage Karen had done on Mum's morning off. Jack was out with India, parenting a pink elephant. I stayed home, did push-ups and got ready for my big date. I told Dad I was going to see *The Elephant Man* with Miranda. I didn't mention her surname.

There were two large pimples on my chin and forehead. I stole a tube of something called "concealer" from Jack's room. It was makeup he used to cover up his own spots. Unfortunately, the concealer was Jack's skin tone (milky coffee) and not mine (goat's cheese). The more concealer I put on, the more my pimples seemed to stand out. In the end I applied a thin layer of the stuff to my whole face. I checked myself out in the mirror and thought I looked pretty good.

Miranda was waiting at the SLC, looking amazing in drill pants and a new singlet. I wore a blue and red shirt with yellow suns that I'd been saving for a special occasion.

"Hi, Carrot."

"Hi, Miranda."

"What's that stuff all over your face?"

"Concealer. To hide my pimples."

"I think I prefer you with pimples."

I must have looked like a wounded puppy. Miranda gave me a quick kiss. It wasn't a full-on pash and we hadn't rolled around like wild animals, because you shouldn't do that in a theater society. But at least it was a beginning.

I wanted to sit in the front row to get a good view of the deformed man. Miranda said she preferred to sit near a fire exit, even though they were the worst seats in the house. We sat and I held Miranda's hand. It felt callused, like mine. It was wonderful to feel our calluses touching. But it was a hot night and our hands got sticky so we unclasped them. It was still amazing to be sitting alongside the girl of my dreams, next to the fire exit.

The Elephant Man is a great play. It's about a man whose head has been hideously deformed by a rare illness. A doctor rescues the man from a freak show, takes him to a hospital and tries to give him a normal life. (This was in the nineteenth century, before makeovers.) I won't give away how the play ends but if you ever see it, take a handkerchief and don't wear concealer.

In the production at the Center you didn't actually see the deformity, which I thought was a cheat at first. But the actor was so good that you could imagine him as a poor, hideous creature. There was a standing ovation at the end, like the one *my* play would probably get.

Most of the people in the audience stayed behind in the foyer. Zoran was there with Mrs. Zoran. I introduced them both to Miranda.

“Set, what did you think of play?” Zoran asked.

“I thought it was good. Especially the deformed man.”

“It is difficult for deformed people in Serbia,” said Zoran.

“Don’t keep on like that,” said Mrs. Zoran. “It is difficult for deformed people everywhere.”

“It is more difficult in Serbia.”

“My husband is idiot,” explained Mrs. Zoran for Miranda’s benefit.

The actor who’d played the lead role appeared, and was instantly surrounded by handsome young men drinking champagne. One of them gave the actor a big bunch of flowers. I saw Zoran’s look of distaste.

“What’s the matter?” I asked.

“I don’t like them,” Zoran said sourly.

“There’s nothing wrong with gay people.”

“I was talking about the flowers.”

“Miranda, what did *you* think of play?” Mrs. Zoran asked.

“Good,” she said. “But it’s a shame they couldn’t afford to do it properly.”

“How do you mean?”

“The deformed man should’ve had a latex head, like in the movies.”

“But couldn’t you imagine big ugly deformed head?” said Mrs. Zoran.

“Not really,” said Miranda. I offered to get Miranda a drink but she said she was okay.

“Set is nice boy,” Mrs. Zoran told her. “So are you,

Miranda. You seem good together. Not like me with Zoran."

I blushed. Zoran moved a little closer to inspect my face. "Set, something is wrong with your skin. Have you been near nuclear reactor?"

"Carrot's wearing makeup," said Miranda.

"You call him Carrot?"

"It's a nickname."

"What is nickname?"

Miranda explained. "It's a sort of *friendly* name."

"We don't have these nicknames in Serbia. If you call someone Carrot, they put you in hospital with electric bars."

"I think Carrot is nice name," Mrs. Zoran said. "Set, do you have nickname for your girlfriend?"

"I just call her Miranda. It's the best name in the world."

"No," said Zoran.

"*My* name is best in world."

"I have nickname for Zoran," Mrs. Zoran confided.

Zoran frowned. "Be quiet, woman, or I will sell you to slave traders."

But Mrs. Zoran told us anyway. I chuckled and Zoran groaned.

"We'd better be going," said Miranda. "It was nice to meet you both."

"Good-bye, Zoozoo," I said. "Good-bye, Mrs. Zoozoo."

Miranda and I walked out into the night. We'd chained up

our bikes so that they wouldn't be stolen by Nanky Rats.

"What's your star sign?" I asked.

"Astrology is crap," said Miranda.

"I agree," I said, because I'm a Libran and we always go with the flow. "Did you mind that Mrs. Zoran thought we were boyfriend and girlfriend?"

Miranda shook her head. "They seem mad anyway."

She was probably a Capricorn because they always speak their minds. Awkward pause.

"It was a good play, Carrot."

"It was great."

"Even without latex."

"Do you want to see another one? Not now, I mean later. What are you doing next weekend?" There was bound to be a play on nearby. We were in the amateur theater belt. It was impossible to go for a jog without running into a production of *The Mikado.*

"I'll ring you," Miranda said.

We were just unchaining our bikes when a huge Mercedes pulled up behind us. We were caught in the glare of its headlights. Miranda looked rattled as she turned to face the car. Someone climbed out and walked slowly toward us, an anonymous silhouette against the glow of quartz halogen. If this had been a Hollywood movie the figure would have shortly abducted us for experiments.

"What is your name?" the person asked. It was Mr. Raven.

I said nothing.

"Young man, what is your name?" Mr. Raven repeated.

"Seth Parrot."

"My daughter is under the impression you're a girl called Tamsin. You're not a girl, are you?"

"No, Mr. Raven."

"You're not called Tamsin?"

"No, Mr. Raven."

"What are you doing with my daughter?"

"We just went to see a play, Mr. Raven. It was very tasteful and there was no bad language."

"Dad ..."

"Please be quiet, Miranda. Young man, I told you to keep away!"

Mr. Raven produced a shifting spanner. He advanced with it and I backed away, in case he wanted to use it as a blunt instrument.

"Get in the car, Miranda. I'm very annoyed with you for lying to me."

"I'll ride my bike home," said Miranda.

"Get in the car immediately!"

Miranda did as she was told. Mr. Raven knelt down and, with the shifting spanner, removed the front wheel of Miranda's bike. He put the wheel and the rest of the bike in the Mercedes' boot. His work done, he turned to me.

"If you dare see my daughter again, the next thing I put in that car boot will be your dead body."

"Yes, Mr. Raven."

I watched the car disappear into the night.

FACT ELEVEN

A niddy noddy is a tool for winding yarn

My relationship with Miranda seemed doomed because our fathers were at war. It was like a classical play. I hoped there'd be no deaths or blindings.

Mum was the only one at home when I returned from *The Elephant Man*. Jack was at Tyrone's pool party and Dad had driven off to pick him up. Mum sat alone in the lounge room with her niddy noddy.

"How was your night?" Mum asked.

"Not great."

"Was it a bad play? I won't let that company use the Center again if it was a bad play."

"No, it was a good play. But things didn't end up being so good with Miranda."

"I'm sorry to hear that, Seth. Niddy noddy niddy noddy," said Mum. (People say this when they use niddy noddies. Strange but true.)

"Are you in love?" Mum asked, between niddy noddies.

"Miranda is the most perfect girl I've ever met."

"I hope we get to meet her one day," said Mum. "Does she love you, too?"

"I don't know. Maybe."

Mum put down her niddy noddy. "Tell me about her."

"She has wonderful quads."

"What else?"

"Her trapezoids are pretty good, too. I couldn't really comment on her rotator cuffs."

"You know, Seth, there's more to a girl than muscles."

"She's also got great cheekbones."

"So what went wrong tonight?"

"I'd prefer not to talk about it."

"Why not?"

"Some things are better left unsaid."

I let Mum complete twelve more niddy noddies.

"Mum, do you still like Dad?" I asked.

"Of course. Your father is a wonderful man."

"Do you *love* him?"

"It's the same thing."

"No it isn't. Penguins like bananas but they don't want to spend their lives with them."

Mum put down her niddy noddy again. "I wish Eric hadn't started this feud with Jeff Raven."

"I don't think he did start it."

"He flicked cow poo at Mr. Raven and didn't apologize."

"He didn't do it deliberately."

"He still should have apologized."

It was terrible to think that such an almighty feud could result from one tiny speck of manure. Did world wars start the same way?

"I'm sure Dad regrets it," I said.

"It's a bit late for that now, isn't it?"

"What do you mean?"

"I'm sorry, Seth." Mum rubbed her eyes. "It's been a tough day. Karen managed to crash all the computers by e-mailing her friends a picture of her cat wearing a dress."

"Dad'll be able to fix that."

"Yes, I suspect he will."

"Is everything all right?"

"Fine," said Mum. "I hope things work out with Miranda. You deserve to have a nice girlfriend. Good night, beautiful boy. Niddy noddy niddy noddy niddy noddy niddy noddy."

I washed off what was left of the concealer and went to bed.

By the time Dad and Jack returned from the party, Mum was asleep in the master bedroom. Dad tried to be as quiet as possible. Jack didn't.

"Isn't it amazing how Tyrone and Kieran can sing all those songs from the movies?" said Jack.

"Yes," said Dad. "Shh."

"I like their house. There's hardly anything in it."

"That's called minimalism. Unless they've been burgled recently."

"Dad, are you in a bad mood?"

"Did you get drunk at the party?"

"No."

"Are you sure?"

"I did have some wine. But that's okay because we have wine at home."

"I don't want you to drink wine at other people's houses. Not until you're a bit older."

"It was only a tiny amount. Most of Tyrone's friends drank buckets of vodka."

"Did India drink wine?"

"Yes, but that isn't what made her throw up."

"What made her throw up?"

"She's a vegetarian and she ate a meat pie."

"She must have been drunk to forget that a meat pie actually contains meat."

"She thought it was a lamington." Jack giggled.

"Are you sure you're not drunk now?"

"Dad, I'm nearly an adult."

"You've betrayed my trust," said Dad. "Go to bed, Jack, and we'll talk about this tomorrow."

Jack came into my bedroom. He did seem drunk.

"I've discovered something about myself," said Jack.

"I already know that you're lactose intolerant," I said. "And that you're color-blind."

"I think I might also be a nudist."

"What? Why?"

"At the party I went swimming with India." Jack's breath stank of green ginger wine. "We took off our bathers. It was brilliant. Can I sit on the bed?"

"No."

Jack sat on the bed. "It's interesting being a nudist. India knows all about it. There are these special camps where you play volleyball or ride bikes in the nude."

“Jack, you’re not a nudist. You’re just drunk.”

Jack burped. “I thought you’d be more tolerant.”

“Okay, okay. If you really are a nudist, then that’s fine with me. Just don’t be one when I’m around. Now get off my bed before I kick you off.”

But Jack wasn’t going anywhere.

“It was a great party. I drank a lot.”

“I can smell it from here.”

“Mr. Banerjee really enjoyed himself.”

“You took your stupid elephant to the party?”

“Our *child*,” Jack corrected me. Then he looked concerned. “I think we might have left him in the pool. I guess that means India and I aren’t very good parents.”

“Did India talk in that little baby voice all night?”

“You’re just jealous. It’s because you haven’t got a girlfriend.”

“I do, actually.”

“I don’t believe you.”

“I went out with her tonight.”

“No girls go for you, except tragic ones.”

“This girl is amazing.”

“Did you pash?”

“Sure.”

“No you didn’t. I can tell when you’re lying. What does she look like? I bet she’s ugly.”

“She’s beautiful.”

“How come we’ve never met her? Are you sure she’s not a boy?”

“Yeah. That’s right. She’s a boy. Miranda’s a boy.”

"Miranda who? What's her last name?"

"I don't have to tell you everything."

"Yes you do. I showed you my tongue stud. Who is she?"

If I told the truth to Jack, he'd immediately tell everyone. And I didn't want Dad to know I was going out with his archenemy's daughter.

"She's from Easter Island," I said. "She builds spiral staircases for a living."

"You're such a loser, Seth. You'll never have a serious girlfriend. Never in a zillion years. If a girl really did go out with you tonight, she probably did it out of sympathy."

"You're a real pain when you're drunk," I said.

"I'm not drunk. I just don't feel very well."

"Go to the bathroom and throw up."

"I don't need to. I've got a strong stomach."

"You know Mr. Kenvyn?" I said.

"What's he got to do with anything?"

"Apparently he's a nudist. You'll probably bump into him when you go to the nudist camp."

Jack ran to the bathroom.

The Sunday edition of the paper had an article about litter-louts. A fisherman had been interviewed about the terrible state of Kinglet River. According to the fisherman, a Mr. Fisher, people had no respect for the environment and were dumping their rubbish anywhere they liked. He was photographed pointing at what appeared to be a state-of-the-art German juice extractor he had caught while fishing for crap. (The newspaper had probably meant to print *carp*.) Mr. Fisher said it was a disgrace that people were disposing of their old carp in this way. (This time the newspaper had probably meant to print *crap*.) In the past month Mr. Fisher had caught a jumper, a toaster and a salad spinner. Mr. Fisher was 47.

Flowerbeds at the Shared Learning Center had also been targeted by litter-louts. A member of the local Serbian community, a Mr. Zoran Krkic Please Check Spelling, said a number of cans and fast-food containers had been dumped in the garden. Mr. Zoran Krkic Please Check Spelling added that "vandal pigs" had pulled up some of the flowers, which he hated. The local Serbian (29) said that in his country of origin people who stole flowers were used instead of monkeys in dangerous lab experiments.

In an unrelated article, Mr. Jeff Raven was happy to announce that the council was very close indeed to finding the cyber-terrorist responsible for the e-mail bomb. There was a photograph of Mr. Raven looking stern and pointing at a computer. Underneath it was a caption: Rubbish found in Kinglet River.

The homemade muesli didn't taste as good as usual. Mum had skimped on the dried fruit. The milk seemed to have been watered down. Dad quietly read the paper. We all crunched away on the disappointing muesli. Jack had a headache and didn't eat as much as usual.

"I'm dying," said Jack.

"Have a glass of water," said Mum.

Jack shook his head, then wished he hadn't.

"How much wine did you have last night?" asked Mum.

"None."

"Then why do you have a headache?"

"I think there was too much chlorine in the pool."

"Well, next time you'll know not to drink pool water."

"Mum, you're not taking me seriously!"

Dad turned a page and said nothing.

"Is anyone concerned?" Jack whined. "I'm really suffering."

"I'm sorry, Jack," said Mum. "I'm sorry you got drunk and that you have a hangover. But there are other things to worry about."

Dad put down the paper. "I'm afraid we won't be going to South Africa."

I was stunned. "Why not?"

"We don't have enough money," said Mum.

"I lost my job on Friday," said Dad.

The muesli felt like sawdust in my mouth.

"But Dad, you're a brilliant I.T. architect."

"Thank you, Seth. And you're a brilliant playwright. And Jack is a brilliant actor. But, at the moment, I'm a brilliant *unemployed* I.T. architect."

"They traced Eric's e-mail bomb back to him," said Mum.

"Mr. Raven was very determined," said Dad. "He spent

a lot of council money on his investigation. I think those Portaloos in his garden pushed him over the edge."

The guilt prickled me and I felt stomach cramps coming on. "But you didn't do it."

"I know," said Dad.

Mum started clearing up the plates. "It doesn't matter who did it. The fact remains that Eric sent that stupid e-mail bomb and now it's blown up in his face."

"Mr. Raven is a fascist!" said Jack.

"He's a Nazi!" I said.

"Stop that!" Mum yelled. "This is the sort of stupid behavior that got us into trouble in the first place!"

Mum angrily carried some plates into the kitchen. Jack got up to help her. He'd never done this before. He knew things were serious.

"You'll be all right, Dad," I said.

"Of course I will, Seth."

"You'll find another job. You can do heaps of things."

"I know. And I was bored with computers anyway."

"You're smart. You could probably become a brain surgeon if you wanted to."

"I could, Seth. Except I don't want to."

"You could be a builder," I said.

"Or a musician," said Dad.

"Or a gardener."

"Or a writer."

I shook my head. "No, Dad, don't be a writer."

Despite my brave face, I was miserable. Dad would be

 able to find another job. I'd never find another girl like Miranda. She drove me mad with desire, but she was becoming more and more unobtainable. Her father hated me. My father hated *her* father. After last night's confrontation, I suspected I'd never hear from Miranda again.

But I did. After breakfast, the phone rang. I grabbed the receiver. I could have sworn I smelled Dencorub coming through it.

"Hi, Carrot."

"Hi, Miranda."

"I'm sorry about last night," said Miranda. "My dad can be difficult."

"Yes."

"If you knew what he'd been through you'd understand."

"I'm sure he has his reasons for behaving the way he does."

I couldn't imagine what they'd be, and Miranda obviously wasn't going to tell me. There was a long pause. A pregnant pause. It very nearly had a baby.

"I had a good time," I said at last. "Apart from the death threat at the end."

"It's a bad time of year for my father," said Miranda.

What did *that* mean? Was it something to do with full moons? He was too bald to be a werewolf.

"Is your dad there now?" I asked.

"He's gone out with the historical society. They're looking at graves. What are *you* up to? Do you want to come over?"

Miranda wanted to get together again—*today.*

"I'm doing nothing," I said. "I mean, I'm obviously doing *something.* I'm on the phone right now talking to you and in a few minutes I'll probably help Dad wash the car, but apart from that I'm totally free to do whatever you want."

"Why don't you come over for lunch?" said Miranda. "Bring your bathers."

"Sure. Is nine thirty too early?"

"Probably for lunch."

"Nine forty-five?"

"Come around at twelve thirty. I'll make sandwiches. Is there anything you can't eat?"

"Fiberglass," I said.

"You're weird, Carrot."

"Good weird or bad weird?"

"What do you think?"

"I'll see you at twelve thirty. Will you hang up first or will I?"

Miranda had already hung up.

FACT TWELVE

A human sheds a complete layer of skin every four weeks

The only bathers I had were my old brief-cut Speedos. These were perfectly good bathers, but of late there'd been a move away from them. This might have been because of all the photos of surf-lifesavers with their tiny Speedos pulled up their cracks, and the understandable reaction from straight boys like me that this was not a good look.

I decided to invest in a new pair of long-cut bathers. The only bathers shop open on Sunday was an expensive one in Kinglet Chase. I tried on eight pairs. The far-too-skinny sales assistant had obviously drunk a lot of coffee, because she was bright and very wide-eyed for a Sunday morning. She kept dancing around to the music, which was Mind Control. She told me that I was a very beautiful person. I think her sales technique was a bit over the top.

I bought a pair of brilliant red bathers that came to just above my knees and cost a hundred times more than what the slave in the overseas sweatshop would have been paid to make them.

I rode my bike to Miranda's house at mach 1, which is the speed of sound (380 meters per second).

Miranda was wearing a sensational new outfit—a babylock black singlet and mattress-stripe pajama shorts. She had amazing style. There was a new picture of a B-2 Spirit Stealth Bomber on the living room wall with all the other planes. It seemed odd that there were so many pictures of airplanes and not a single one of Miranda's mother. Surely she can't have been ugly?

Miranda and I paddled around in the pool. A crow went *caw!* because it was sick and tired of bellbirds getting all the attention. I hadn't told Miranda about Dad losing his job and wasn't sure if she knew.

"Are they new bathers?" asked Miranda.

"Yes."

"Red suits you. It matches your hair."

"And yellow suits you. It matches your letterbox."

"You're being weird again, Carrot."

"Sorry, Miranda."

"I don't mind. It's good weird."

The world seemed perfect. I was in love, Miranda was in a swimsuit and her father was in a cemetery. The water was buoyant and beautiful. The ghost gums gave off their robust eucalyptus scent. Churchill grazed on some grass and was quietly sick.

"Miranda, can you please get a mobile phone?" I said.

"Dad won't let me have one. He thinks they cause fires."

"That's just a dumb urban myth."

"My father is very nervous about fires. And please don't ring here or he'll chuck a fit."

"What if I disguise my voice?"

"Are you good at disguising your voice?"

I did my best Indian accent.

"Don't ring here," Miranda said.

"Okay. But you have to ring me. Every day. Promise."

"I promise."

"Otherwise I'll think something terrible has happened to you, like falling down a mine. I have a vivid imagination."

"I guess that's good, if you're going to write plays."

The last thing I wanted to think about was my stupid play. I hated the idea of rewriting it, even though it no longer seemed quite as good as I'd first thought. Poppy was right. All the characters *did* sound the same.

Miranda and I floated on our backs and admired the white moon in the clear blue sky.

"Isn't it surprising that our moon is the only one that doesn't have a name?" I said. "We just call it *moon*. That's like me calling you *girl*."

"Or me calling you *dag*," said Miranda, sweetly.

"And planet Earth is the only one in the solar system that isn't named after a god."

"That's interesting."

"Do you like my interesting facts?"

"Where do you get them all?"

"From my dad. Did you hear about my dad?"

"What about him?"

Miranda didn't seem to know that he'd been sacked. We stopped floating and faced each other.

"He's getting a new job," I lied. It was only a white lie.

"What sort of job?"

"It's a promotion. He's going to earn heaps more money."

"What will he be doing?"

"Working for the government."

"Doing what?"

"Code-breaking." The white lie was rapidly turning gray. "We may even have to move interstate."

Miranda looked thoughtful. "I'd probably miss you if you moved interstate."

"I'd miss you, too."

Another gum leaf fell into the pool. Miranda picked it up and examined it as though it were the most fascinating gum leaf in the world.

"They have gum trees in California," I said.

Miranda put her finger to my lips before I could mention any more interesting facts about gum trees. When she took her hand away, I felt as if an electric charge had run through my whole body.

"Will you be my serious girlfriend?" I asked.

Miranda dropped the leaf and moved toward me. We kissed for about a century and a thousand bellbirds went *ping!*

We had lunch. I'd happily have eaten fiberglass sandwiches for Miranda. But the ham and cheese ones were excellent. We spent the whole afternoon together. Miranda said I had the best abdominals she'd ever seen. I made flattering comments about her soleus muscles. Miranda taught me some acrobatics. My favorite one was keeping my body rigid so that I could balance on Miranda's feet, as she lay on her back and held up her legs.

I left at six o'clock, because Miranda's dad would be home by seven. I was deliriously happy. Luck had finally come my way. I'd spent Sunday afternoon with a girl who made Opal Honey look like a badly morphed horse. It seemed likely I had a serious girlfriend.

On the way home, George Jupitus ambushed me and punched the crap out of me.

FACT THIRTEEN

During its life an oyster changes its sex several times

I not only had a fat lip, I also had a squashed ear and I was experiencing a ringing noise that had nothing to do with bellbirds.

Dad was spraying some sort of chemical on the lemon tree when I got home. The plastic spray pack had an insanely grinning gnome on the label.

"Hello, Seth."

"Hi, Dad."

The sun was behind me so Dad didn't immediately notice my fat lip.

"Did you have a good day?" Dad asked.

"Yes and no."

"Tell me about the *yes* bit." The chemical stank. Dad continued to spray it at the base of the tree.

"I think I may now have a serious girlfriend," I said.

"I told you it'd happen." Dad was pleased. "Presumably this is the Miranda girl?"

"Yes," I said. "The Miranda girl."

"I can't wait to meet her."

"This brings me to the *no* part of the day," I said. "I've just been assaulted."

Dad dropped the chemical spray pack and had a good look at my face. He moved me around so that the sun caught my fat lip.

"It probably looks worse than it is," I said.

"I'll get you to a doctor."

"I'm okay. It doesn't hurt that much."

"Come inside and I'll fix you up."

"Really, Dad, I'm okay."

"I still want you to come inside with me."

"I don't want to go inside, Dad. I want you to help me practice my jumpkicks."

"Not now, Seth."

"I think now would be a really good time."

"Tell me what happened."

"I'll tell you later, after the jumpkicks." I picked up the spray pack. The gnome on the bottle looked evil. "What's this? What is high-nitrogen-potassium formula?"

"I've decided to stop peeing on the lemon tree," Dad said. "Zilla didn't like it. I'm using a product with the same ingredients."

"You *paid* for this?"

"Of course I did."

"Why did you pay for wee?"

"It's not wee. At least I hope it's not. I'd hate to think I paid Mr. Racina twenty-five dollars for a bottle of wee."

"This container doesn't look biodegradable," I said. "Mum won't be pleased."

"I'm finding it rather difficult to please Zilla at the moment, Seth. She's off visiting her mother."

A bellbird gave a sympathetic *ping!*

"Could we do the jumpkicks, Dad? It'd make me feel better."

Dad sighed. "If you like, Seth."

He went to fetch the pad from the shed.

Dad seemed surprised by how hard I was kicking.

"Don't be so violent," he said. "This is meant to be exercise, not combat."

I recalled George Jupitus punching me and putting me in a headlock. I kicked even harder.

"Do you want to take a breather?" Dad asked, after a while.

"Just a few more minutes."

Jack ran out to join us, dressed in neck-to-knee Lycra. I hoped he was wearing underpants. I didn't want a repeat of his last performance.

"One at a time," Dad yelled. "One at a time."

"I want a go," said Jack.

Jack kicked and kicked. But I wasn't going to bow out and let him take over, like last time. I kicked higher and harder than ever. Next door, Mr. Robbins applauded one of my better efforts. I turned around to show my appreciation.

Never turn around when you're in the middle of a jumpkick frenzy. One tiny lapse of concentration can lead to serious injury. You might do terrible damage to yourself. You might even do terrible damage to your little brother.

I sideswiped Jack's head with a badly timed jumpkick.

Jack fell to the ground. He lay still, like a circus acrobat who'd fallen from a high wire. Neither Dad nor I spoke. I felt sick. Had I become the Seth of Egyptian mythology? Had I murdered my brother? Finally, Jack groaned.

"Jack. Are you all right?" said Dad.

Jack looked dazed. His eyes were wide.

"I think I need to lie down," said Jack.

"You *are* lying down," I said.

"Then I think I need to sit up."

Dad and I helped Jack to sit up. There was no blood. There wasn't even any bruising. But I'd kicked my brother in the head with considerable force. I was terrified that I might have damaged his brain.

"Does it hurt?" I asked.

"Does what hurt?" asked Jack.

"Your brain."

Jack moved his head around to see if his brain hurt. He didn't seem to be in any pain.

"How do you feel, Jack?" asked Dad.

"Who's Jack?" said Jack.

"Come on, Jack," said Dad. "We're taking you to the doctor."

Mum had taken the car to visit Gran. Dad asked Mr. Robbins if he could borrow his Holden Astra to drive Jack to the doctor. Of course Mr. Robbins handed over the keys immediately. "Take it," he said.

We bundled Jack into the car. He looked perfectly serene and untroubled. As Dad drove the car to the hospital, I kept asking Jack questions to work out the extent of the damage.

"Jack, do you know who the deputy prime minister is?"

"No."

He was in bad shape.

"Jack, do you know what the capital of New Zealand is?"

"No."

"Are you sure? Please, Jack, think!"

"I have no idea," said Jack.

My brother was brain-damaged and it was all my fault. I'd turned him into a vegetable. A salad ingredient.

"Ask him some other questions," said Dad. "I don't think Jack knew the answers to those ones even *before* you kicked him."

"Jack, what is the name of the makeup that covers pimples?" I asked.

"Concealer," said Jack.

"What is Botox?"

"It's stuff to get rid of wrinkles."

Now we were making progress.

"And what do you call the things that make boobs bigger?"

"Implants," said Jack. "Or push-up bras."

"You're going to be all right!" I cried.

"Can I ask a question?" said Jack. "Who are you?"

Oh God. He was going to be a vegetable after all.

The four of us sat in Dr. Penhaligon's surgery, surrounded by medical clutter. Dr. Penhaligon had been called away from a Sunday barbecue and was a little flustered. He shone a torch in my eyes.

"He's not the patient," said Dad.

"Then what's all this?" asked Dr. Penhaligon, indicating my fat lip and facial bruising.

"I was assaulted," I explained. "But I'm fine. Jack's the one we're worried about."

"What's happened to Jack?"

"I kicked him in the head," I said.

Dr. Penhaligon turned to Dad. "Is this correct?"

"There was a kickboxing accident," Dad said. "Seth didn't do it deliberately."

"Implants," said Jack, peacefully. "Push-up bras."

I swallowed hard. "I think I might have damaged his brain."

Dr. Penhaligon seemed uncomfortable that Jack was dressed in shiny aqua Lycra, but didn't say anything. He briefly examined Jack with his torch. Finally, Dr. Penhaligon advised that he wouldn't know if any damage had been done until he looked at Jack's brain. The peaceful expression on Jack's face changed.

"How will you do that?" Jack asked.

"I'll send you to get something called a C.T. scan. It's a kind of brain x-ray."

"Will it hurt?" Jack seemed surprisingly alert all of a sudden.

"It won't hurt. All that happens is you lie on a nice padded bench, which slides into an enormous electronic doughnut. This doughnut clicks and whirrs and takes an x-ray of your brain."

"What's a doughnut?" asked Jack.

We had to drive Jack to Gang Gang General Hospital. In the radiology department Jack had his brain scanned for immediate analysis by Dr. Penhaligon. It was probably the first time the staff had given a C.T. scan to someone dressed like a member of Cirque du Soleil.

Dr. Penhaligon gave us the wonderful news that there appeared to be nothing whatever wrong with Jack's brain. We should contact him, however, if Jack started acting strangely.

In the car on the way back to Jacana Avenue, Jack kept pointing at objects and asking me what they were.

"That's a tree, Jack," I said.

"And what's that?"

"That's another tree."

I wasn't sure if Jack was pretending or not, but I decided to give him the benefit of the doubt.

"What's that thing over there?" he asked.

"That's a house, Jack. That's where you live."

Mum had arrived from Gran's. We returned the Holden Astra to Mr. Robbins, who'd already filled Mum in on some of the details. When we told her the full story, Mum gave a long and exhausted sigh. Jack kept pointing at things and asking what they were.

That night, Mum decided to cancel the kickboxing classes

at the Center. They were obviously too dangerous. It was the *last* time she'd bow to public pressure. When she asked me what had happened to my lip I told her it was a cold sore. She didn't notice my bruised cheek. I'd used more of Jack's concealer to disguise it. I hadn't bothered to ask Jack. If he really *was* brain-damaged, he wouldn't realize anyway.

Dinner was take-away Chinese food. Mum didn't seem to care that the plastic containers were non-biodegradable. Jack's vocabulary returned enough for him to ask for a second helping of ginger beef with bean shoots. Dad tried to lighten the mood by revealing an interesting fact. He'd read somewhere that the ancient Egyptians taught baboons to be waiters. Mum's response was that baboons were obviously better at learning things than some humans she knew.

After dinner, I took the Mr. Right list off my wall. I folded it up carefully and placed it in Dad's toothbrush mug.

Very late that night, when I was in bed, the phone rang. Jack ran out of his bedroom to pick up the receiver.

"Hello?" he said. "I think this is Jack here."

The person at the other end spoke.

"What is a Miranda?" said Jack. "Who is Seth? I don't think there's anyone here called Seth."

The person at the other end said something else.

"You sound kind of sexy," said Jack, becoming magically clear-headed.

Another comment from the person at the other end.

"Why do you want to talk to Seth when you could talk to me?"

I grabbed the phone and told Jack to go back to bed. He asked what a bed was.

"Hi, Carrot."

"Hi, Miranda. Sorry, that was just my brother."

"He sounds like a pain."

"No, he's charismatic and everyone loves him."

"He doesn't seem charismatic on the phone."

Obviously Jack's charisma only worked on a visual level.

How could I tell Miranda all the news? I decided to start with the positive stuff first.

"I had a good time today, Miranda."

"So did I, Carrot."

"Especially the acrobatic balancing."

"I enjoyed it, too."

"Next time you have to balance on *my* legs."

"I'll look forward to that."

I took a deep breath. Now it was time to tackle the negative stuff.

"I got bashed up by George Jupitus," I said.

"What?"

"And I kicked Jack in the head."

"*What?*"

"And Mum has decided to cancel the kickboxing course at the Center."

"Carrot, could we go through these things one at a time?" Miranda was speaking in hushed tones. Her father was obviously at the house.

"Well, on the way home from your place, I got bashed up by George."

"Tell the police," said Miranda.

"No."

"Why not? He's a thug! Are you badly hurt?"

"Just a fat lip. It's already slimming down."

"I feel bad about this."

"You shouldn't." I tried to collect my thoughts. "Miranda, when I asked if you were my serious girlfriend, you never actually said yes or no. And I just want you to know that I'm very happy to be your serious boyfriend. I'd do anything for you. I'd swim across rivers. I'd climb the Atlas Mountains. Even the underwater ones."

"Carrot, could you slow down please? You told me three things before and they were fairly big things so I think we should deal with those first," said Miranda. "I can't talk for long."

"Of course, I understand."

"What happened to Jack?"

Miranda was treating the phone conversation as though there were an agenda. *Item 1. Jack kicked in head.* "How did you kick your brother?" she asked.

"I accidentally knocked him out with an inside jump-kick."

"That's not good. Is he okay?"

"He says he keeps forgetting stuff but I think it might be a con."

"I heard that," called Jack from his bedroom.

"Stop eavesdropping," I yelled.

"Rude gestures!" Jack yelled back.

"Rude gestures to the power of ten!" Then I lowered my voice. "Sorry, Miranda, I probably should've covered the receiver when I did that."

Item 2. Kickboxing classes canceled.

"Why did your mum cancel the classes?" Miranda asked.

I told her it probably had a lot to do with item 1 on the agenda.

"There are heaps of other courses you could do," I added. "There's a good Tai Chi one. I think you have to be pregnant but you could fake it. And there's Asian cookery, which can be interesting. And you don't have to be pregnant for that."

"I'm really only interested in kickboxing," said Miranda.

"I'm sorry about that."

"It's probably just as well. Dad's bound to find out if I keep hanging around the Center. It might get ugly."

"He bosses you around too much," I said.

"He's not as bad as you think, Carrot."

I didn't want to tell her that her father made Predator look like Pingu.

Item 3. Miscellaneous.

"So when will I see you again?" I asked.

"Soon, I hope."

"We'll have to make a time and a place. A secret place."

"What about *your* place?"

"Things are quite stressful here at the moment, now that Dad's unemployed."

"I thought you said he was getting a promotion?"

Damn! "Yes, I did say that. But the demand for code-breakers seems to have dried up all of a sudden."

There was a crackling noise and a third voice joined our conversation. Miranda's house had two phones!

"Get off the phone, Miranda," said Mr. Raven. "It's late."

"I'm just talking to someone."

"Hello, I'm Tamsin," I squeaked.

"I know who you are, young man."

"Did you enjoy the graves, Mr. Raven?" I asked, trying to charm him. *Never give up without a fight. Remember rule twenty-one.*

"I did enjoy the graves," said Mr. Raven. "Though I'd have enjoyed them more if you and your father had been in them."

"Dad! Seth's having a bad time. His father's just lost his job."

"I know. I'm proud to be the one who lost it for him. Now get lost, young man, before I come around with an AK-47!"

"Well, nice talking to you, Mr. Raven," I said. "Good-bye, Miranda."

"Good-bye, Carrot."

"Do not call again, young man," said Mr. Raven. "Do not send letters. Do not send carrier pigeons. Do not attempt any form of communication whatever or I'll run over you."

I hung up, a victim of road rage by phone. At least Miranda now had a better idea of what was going on.

FACT FOURTEEN

A pregnant goldfish is called a twit

On Monday Jack stayed home from school. He rang India to tell her what had happened. It was a long conversation because Jack kept forgetting words. He told India I'd kicked him in the head and ruined his vocabulary. Only it took him a long time to remember the word *vocabulary*. Jack asked India what the hole in the wall was, the one he could look out of and see the front garden. On the other end of the line, India would have tearfully told him that this was called a *window*.

India came around and gave Jack a little furry toy wombat. He asked what it was. She told him it was called a teddy bear. India should never be employed as a teacher. She gave me a look of hatred as she sat down with a picture book she'd brought to help Jack get back his vocabulary.

"Bah-lamb," said India, pointing to a picture of an angora goat.

"Bah-lamb," repeated Jack.

On his first day of being unemployed, Dad worked harder than ever. He made a new niddy noddy for Mum. He constructed a brand new letterbox. It was nowhere near as impressive as the old one, but it looked strong enough to survive a meteorite shower. He also made sure that it didn't stick out over the footpath.

Miranda rang on Monday night to tell me she hadn't fallen down any mines. I told her I liked her adductor muscles. She told me she liked my glutes. When I started listing the mountains I'd climb for her she said there was no time for that stuff and she had to go. She'd ring me again on Tuesday night.

"Are you my serious girlfriend?" I asked, just before she hung up.

I'm pretty sure she said, "Yes, Carrot, I'm your serious girlfriend, and I will love you forever," although it wasn't a good connection.

Dad slept on the couch in the front room.

On his second day of being unemployed, Dad built a new Web site for the SLC and fixed all the computers Karen had crashed. He convinced her that the photocopier was her friend and that she needn't be frightened of it.

I dropped in to Franca's Hair and Legs to ask Franca for a special favor. She sighed and said a whole lot of stuff in Italian about young love. She'd do anything for me, she said. She still felt guilty about my ear.

Miranda rang on Tuesday night to tell me she still hadn't

been in any mine accidents. I told her to get a pet dog to take with her when she went orienteering in the foothills. Churchill was a nice cat, but he'd be no use to her in a mine accident. I told her I'd found a secret place where we could meet. We made a date for Thursday night. I told Miranda I admired her gastrocnemius muscle. She told me she liked my sternocleidomastoids.

Dad slept on the couch in the front room.

On his third day of being unemployed, Dad helped Zoran with the garden at the SLC, teaching him the Latin names of some of the flowers. Zoran said he would never remember them because he hated the flowers so much.

"I'd like to teach carpentry," said Dad at dinner that night.

"What is carpentry?" asked Jack.

"It's the craft of working with wood," said Dad, who was being very patient about Jack's disability.

"What is wood?" asked Jack.

"Shut up," I said, less patiently than Dad.

"I'm not sure if I can employ you, Eric," said Mum. "People would say it was nepotism."

"What is nepotism?" asked Jack.

I told Jack to shut up again. Dad told me it was quite likely that Jack honestly didn't know the meaning of the word *nepotism*.

"It means employing someone just because they're

related to you and not based on any skills they have," said Mum.

"It wouldn't be nepotism because I'm a good carpenter and I'll teach the class for nothing," said Dad. "And now that you have a group of big strong boys with no kick-boxing class to attend, it might be good to give them something to occupy their time."

Dad managed to convince Mum. He would start teaching the classes on Thursday night, the night after drama class. I was meeting Miranda on Thursday night but I still signed up for Dad's class. I'd see Miranda straight after hammering and sawing. It'd work out well. I'd be masculine and pumped and sweaty.

When we finished dinner, Dad handed a flat brown package to Mum.

"This arrived for you today," he said.

Mum removed the wrapping. It was an old-fashioned vinyl record called *Teaser and the Firecat*. There was an autograph on the cover: Cat Stevens.

"Eric, where did you get this?"

"I found it on eBay."

Mum kept staring at the record cover, with its picture of a vagabond boy and his bright orange cat.

"Did it cost much?"

"Not really."

"I won't be able to play it."

"Yes you will," said Dad. "I reconnected the old turntable."

•

Later that night I crept down to the bathroom for a pee. A warm, crackling version of "Moonshadow" was playing. Mum and Dad were in the front room, sitting together with their eyes closed, listening. Mum was holding her new niddy noddy, but her hands were still.

In the drama class Will Stretton reminded me curtly that rehearsals of my play would start soon and that a new draft was needed as soon as possible. Will knew that I'd signed up for Dad's carpentry class and was annoyed with me for two-timing. Everyone was sad to hear of Jack's problem with forgetting words. We played drama games where we didn't have to speak or think, so Jack wouldn't feel left out.

On Wednesday night I waited for Miranda to ring, but she didn't. It was already ten o'clock and I hadn't heard from her. What had happened? Had there been some terrible accident? Was she in a hospital ward somewhere with tubes up her nose, surrounded by people in white coats gravely shaking their heads?

At 10:23 I decided I'd have to ring Miranda at home, even though she'd asked me not to. The phone rang three times before someone picked up.

"Hello?" It was Jeff Raven. Damn! "Who is this?"

I put on my best Indian accent. "My name is Mr. Banerjee."

"What do you want, Mr. Banerjee?"

"I am a teacher at your daughter Miranda's school and

I would like to talk to her."

"What is this about? Is there a problem?"

"There is no problem. I am just ringing to congratulate her on writing a brilliant essay. Is Miranda all right, by the way?"

"She is perfectly all right."

"I am very relieved to hear it and give thanks to Ganesha."

"Are you in the habit of ringing your students at home, Mr. Banerjee?" asked Mr. Raven.

"Only the good ones," I said. "May I speak with Miranda, please?"

"Mr. Banerjee, your accent is a little hard to place. Where are you from, exactly?"

"Mumbai."

"You don't sound like any Indian I've heard before."

"I have a cold."

"Mr. Banerjee, would I be right in presuming you're that stupid Parrot boy?"

"I am most sorry, I seem to have a wrong number," I said, hanging up.

This was not Mr. Right behavior. Mr. Right would never put on a bad Indian accent to fool his girlfriend's father.

I dialed again, determined to make amends. This time I got an answering machine with one of those stupid computer messages. "*We are un-able to an-swer the tele-phone at the mom-ent. Ple-ase le-ave your na-me, mes-sage and num-ber af-ter the be-ep.*" Mr. Raven obviously wasn't taking any more calls that night. I was about to hang up, but something made me speak. It was probably rule twenty-one.

"Hello, Mr. Raven, this is Seth Parrot speaking. That was me before. I'm sorry I pretended to be Indian but sometimes love makes you do ridiculous things. It makes you think about someone the whole time, to the point that you worry about them whenever you hear about planes crashing or ferries sinking, even if they haven't been on any planes or ferries recently. I was ringing to make absolutely sure that Miranda wasn't in hospital with tubes up her nose. It's a huge relief to know she isn't. I'd rather be in an iron lung than for Miranda to have just one tiny tube up her nose. I'm also really, really sorry my dad flicked manure at you and also that I was rude to you, but that was because I also love my dad and he was upset, so I wasn't thinking straight. Life is too short to bear grudges, Mr. Raven. Most humans don't live for longer than ninety years and that really isn't much time when you consider that a Galápagos tortoise can live to over three hundred. If there's anything I can do to correct the mistakes of the past, just name it and I'll do it. I love your daughter and it isn't just physical and I swear I haven't been very physical with her anyway. I love everything about her and I think she feels the same way about me. Oscar Wilde said that a life without love is like a sunless garden where the flowers are dead, and he really knew his stuff. And furthermore ..."

There was another beep. The machine had run out of recording time.

Miranda rang me very late on Wednesday night to tell me she couldn't talk for long and *please* not to ring her house again! Her dad had been in a furious mood. I asked Miranda if it was because of my answering machine message, and Miranda said their machine had been broken for weeks. Apparently I'd dialed a wrong number and left my message of undying love on someone else's answering machine. I told Miranda I liked her sartorius muscle. She told me she liked my hamstrings. We would still meet tomorrow. Miranda said she couldn't wait.

On Thursday Jack and India made an incredible discovery. While India was helping Jack to get his vocabulary back, they discovered they were telepathic. All India had to do was think of an animal and Jack could almost always tell what it was. Since it was usually an elephant, this didn't amaze me as much as it amazed them.

The students in Dad's carpentry class were mainly teenage boys, who got on well with him. They liked his odd sense of humor, though they weren't so crazy about some of the interesting facts. Only one of the students was a girl. She had a tooth missing, flabby arms and a slightly fuzzy face. She was a Nanky Rat and she smoked. Her name was Elizabeth Taylor. Elizabeth fancied me, I could tell. She kept looking across at me and using the bradawl in a suggestive way. I didn't like it. Now I knew what girls felt like when boys perved at them. I decided never to perve at girls again unless I couldn't help it.

All the kids knew that Dad had lost his regular job because of Mr. Raven. A slightly deaf boy called Damon, who always yelled, said he'd also had a bad experience with Mr. Raven. Damon and his father had set up a hotdog stand outside their house, but Mr. Raven had made them close it down. Damon had been so angry he'd thrown a balloon full of water at Mr. Raven, though he'd missed and hit a cat.

Some kids hung around after the class to talk with Dad. I raced off to a top secret romantic meeting with Miranda.

FACT FIFTEEN

Your hair does not, in fact, keep growing after you die

Franca had put on Frank Sinatra because she said it was more romantic than harp music. The salt crystal lamp gave off a warm glow. The rain forests in the pictures looked perfect for orienteering. Dressed in a dark blue ladies' shimmel and famous-brand linear shorts, Miranda was already waiting for me on one of the chaise longues. I was wearing a sweaty polo shirt and my new red boardies. I could see Miranda was impressed. The beauty room at Franca's Hair and Legs was all ours for the next forty-five minutes.

"You two behave yourselves!" said Franca as she gently closed the door and went off to attend to customers. Miranda brushed her hair back behind her ears.

"Cool place," she said.

"You like it?"

Miranda nodded. "What's it for?"

"Waxing ladies," I said.

"I never got waxed before."

"You don't need waxing. I like the blonde hairs on your arms and legs."

Miranda smiled. "I like yours, too. You look sweaty."

"Thanks. So do you."

"Thanks."

We fell into each other's arms and pashed like mad as Frank Sinatra sang a song about how he was flying to the moon. He mentioned Jupiter and Mars. He was obviously taking a fairly roundabout route. As Miranda and I embraced, I felt the muscles moving in her back: the serratus, the posticus, the inferior. I saw stars and fireworks and Chinese dragons and girls doing the butterfly.

Franca knocked on the door. "Quiet in there."

Miranda and I disengaged. I hadn't realized we'd been making noises. Franca opened the door a smidgeon.

"The customers can hear you. I told them it was someone being waxed but they didn't believe me."

"Sorry, Franca," I said.

"That's okay, *caro mio.* Would you like a cup of coffee?"

Neither Miranda nor I wanted a cup of coffee. The phone rang in the salon. Franca smiled, put her finger to her lips and closed the door.

"We should probably talk about what's going on," I said. "We can't just keep meeting here in the beauty room. Franca has her waxing business to think of."

"What do you suggest we do?"

"We need to tell our dads we're in a serious relationship," I said. "They'll just have to cope with it, no matter how badly they get along."

"My dad hated George," said Miranda.

"Well, that's understandable."

"But he seems to hate you more. And your father."

"How do you think we'll reconcile our dads?"

"Well," said Miranda, "I think your dad should apologize to mine."

"But my dad didn't start it."

"My dad says he did."

"But he didn't. I was there. I saw."

"My dad isn't a liar, Seth."

Seth? The fireworks stopped going off. The girls doing the butterfly ran into difficulty.

"I'm not saying he's a liar, Miranda. But he is very officious. You have to admit that."

"He has to deal with a lot of difficult people. We have to keep changing our phone number because he gets threats."

"I bet he does."

Miranda was annoyed. "Seth!"

Outside, Franca was starting to raise her voice as she spoke on the phone. Italian insults permeated the beauty room.

"*Vincenzo! Non me ne importa un cavolo!*"

"I'm sorry, Miranda. I'm sorry I said that stuff about your dad. I think being in love makes people stupid."

"You're not stupid," said Miranda. "Sometimes you're just a bit …"

Miranda couldn't find the word.

"What? What am I?"

"Intense. Just relax. You're fine when you relax."

"Okay, I'll relax."

Outside, Franca's phone call was making her angrier and angrier.

"It really does upset my father when you call at home," said Miranda.

"I'm sorry about that. It's just that I'm so crazy about you."

"I like you too, Seth."

Seth again! The girls who'd been doing the butterfly were now floating on the surface of the pool and paramedics had been called.

"Miranda," I said, "would you mind calling me Carrot instead of Seth? Because it's sort of freaking me out that you're not."

"Sorry, Carrot."

"And I really need to ask you a question."

"Sure."

"Are you my serious girlfriend?"

"Well ..."

"Well, what?"

"Relax, Carrot!"

"Yes or no? It shouldn't be that hard to answer. Do you *love* me?"

"Carrot, I really, really, really *like* you. I don't think we're serious boyfriend and girlfriend just yet."

I was devastated. The paramedics were applying defibrillators to the butterfly girls. "Liking me isn't enough. Anyone can like. Amoebas can like. Plants can like."

"I like you a *lot*."

"And penguins like bananas."

"What?"

"It's just an interesting fact my dad told me. I like my dad. He's a good guy."

"Seth, he sent my father an e-mail bomb. He wrote a letter in the local paper describing him as a chromus domus. He even sent six portable toilets to our home!"

I swallowed. "He didn't send the toilets."

"Of course he did."

"He didn't."

"Then who did?"

I'd kept it bottled up for long enough. Rule six on the Mr. Right list kept knocking on my conscience. It was disturbing my sleep. It was even more important than rule twenty-one.

"I did," I said. "I sent the Portaloos."

"*What?*"

"I know I've been saying sorry quite a lot lately, but this is the biggest sorry of all. I don't know what came over me. I've regretted it every single day. But I'm the one who committed credit fraud with your dad's card. I'll pay back whatever it cost. And I'll do anything to make it up to you and your father."

"Those Portaloos drove him crazy." Miranda jumped off the chaise longue and started pacing around the beauty room. "You psycho, Seth! I love my father."

"Then I think you should do him a favor," I said. "I think you should tell him to back off."

"You don't know anything about my dad."

The words came tumbling out of me. "I know it'll be

hard for you, but I think you should stand up to him."

"It's nothing to do with you."

"I guess not," I said, "since you're not my serious girlfriend."

No survivors. A freak butterfly accident. All ten swimmers horribly electrocuted when the pool was struck by ball lightning.

Franca, flushed with rage, opened the door of the beauty room and told us we had to leave. Vincenzo had dumped her again. She intended to cut off his *pisello* with scissors. Miranda said she was just going anyway.

The weekend passed agonizingly slowly. Dad made a bookshelf for all the books that Mum had already sent away to the Brotherhood, which shows how pointless life can be. Mum kept playing the Cat Stevens record over and over. What did the words mean anyway? What the hell was a "Moonshadow" and why was it so keen on following Cat Stevens around? It was obviously some sort of stalker.

I read a moronic play by some idiot called Ionesco. It was about a bunch of people who turn into rhinoceroses for no reason. Why do people *write* stuff like this?

Jack's vocabulary returned fully. He discovered that not only were he and India telepathic, they were psychokinetic. They'd both stared at a cup and it had slid three centimeters across the table because of their mental powers. Mental was right.

I didn't try to contact Miranda and I certainly didn't ride my bike over to her house to see if I could catch a glimpse of her statuesque form, because that would have been unbalanced "Moonshadow" behavior. Miranda didn't love me. She'd only ever *liked* me. And now she probably hated me.

Poppy brought photos of her brand-new puppy to drama class. She hadn't thought of a name for it yet. Will Stretton turned it into a drama game: *Name Poppy's Dog.* Casper and Jasper suggested Psycho. Nangret said Clover was a lucky name. (Nangret didn't have a clue. She'd called her guinea pig Princess Diana.) Tyrone suggested Madonna, Jack and India suggested Tinky Winky, I suggested Cerberus the Hound of Hell and Lukas suggested nothing.

Will Stretton kept on at me about how my second draft was going, and I told him I was thinking about putting a lot more killing in the play. Everyone except for Casper and Jasper thought this was a bad idea.

I walked by the old kickboxing room, which was now full of women making dried flower arrangements. It's amazing what rubbish some people do in their spare time. None of the women had impressive shoulders like Miranda. Not that I was thinking about her. That was over. It had never really started.

At dinner when Jack asked me to pass the vegetable salt, I told him to use his bloody psychokinesis and get it himself. Dad told me not to snap at my brother. Jack gave me a self-satisfied look.

"Mum, Dad, I think you should know that Jack has a tongue-stud," I said.

"No I don't!" Jack wore a look of panic.

"Oh, for heaven's sake, your father and I are not complete idiots," said Mum. "We've already noticed that hideous thing in your mouth, Jack."

"Why didn't you say anything?"

"You can't always be the center of attention. Sometimes there are other things to worry about."

"We'll still love you even if we hate that disgusting tongue-stud," said Dad.

Jack was angry. "It's not disgusting."

"It is," said Mum.

"You're prosecuting me for being individual."

"Persecuting," said Mum.

Jack was by now quite worked up. "I'll get a nose stud and a lip stud. I'll tell everyone at the Center your real name is Barbara."

Mum just shrugged. "I was thinking of changing it back anyway."

"Not hungry, Seth?" asked Dad.

"No."

The carpentry students stayed back to chat with Dad after his class on Thursday night. They were concerned he'd go to jail for sending the e-mail bomb. Dad reassured them that if he went to court, he'd probably just end up doing community service. I was making a pig's breakfast of my miter joint.

"Do you want a hand with that, Seth?" Dad asked.

"No."

Elizabeth Taylor and two of the other students in the carpentry class made a brand-new sign for the Center. It was beautifully carved and painted, even if the spelling wasn't great. The old one was warped and peeling, and needed replacing. Dad said that this new sign was excellent, but the Currawong Council mightn't approve because it was rather big.

"Currawong Council sucks," Elizabeth Taylor said.

I rode my bike past Miranda's house to see if I could at least get a glimpse of my lost love. All I glimpsed was Mr. Raven hosing the garden. When he saw me lingering he turned the hose on me. At least it wasn't an AK-47.

By now Miranda would have told her father that I was the credit card criminal. It was just a matter of time before the long arm of the law caught up with me.

FACT SIXTEEN

Grasshoppers hear with their legs

Saturday morning was golden, and the bellbirds were going berserk. The sign on the front of the SLC was beautifully carved and painted, a real labor of love. It was clearly visible from the road and the sun glinted off the bright letters. It read: CURRAWONG COUNSEL SUX.

By the time Mum arrived at the SLC, Jeff Raven was already there with a building inspector, making a list. Mum tried to explain that the sign was erected without her knowing, that she had no idea who was responsible. Mr. Raven barely acknowledged her.

It wasn't Dad's fault that his students had made the sign. You could tell he had nothing to do with it, because he'd have made sure the spelling was correct. But there was fire in Mum's eyes when she came home.

"Mr. Raven and his colleagues have closed down the Center!" Mum announced. "I'll call the media! I'll ring that brown boobies man!"

"I don't think that brown boobies man is still on TV," said Dad.

"This is petty bureaucracy at its worst," said Mum.

“The Shared Learning Center provides work and hope for hundreds of people. And Seth’s play won’t be performed.”

I no longer cared about my play.

“The SLC is the heart and soul of Kinglet,” said Mum. “We must fight against Mr. Raven.”

“I still don’t think that brown boobies man is on TV,” said Dad.

Jack and I were both excused from school because Mum said we were required to help wage war against petty bureaucracy. Our principal gave permission for us to stay home, but only if the war against petty bureaucracy didn’t go on for longer than a day. Mum spent the morning on the phone. I provided backup, such as wheatgrass juice, herbal tea and pens. Jack and India helped with the power of their minds.

I was getting over Miranda. I couldn’t even remember exactly what she looked like. Fighting the war against petty bureaucracy was all I needed to forget the olive-skinned, brown-haired, green-eyed goddess in harem pants.

Meanwhile, Dad drove to the SLC and removed the sign that had offended Mr. Raven and his friends. Then he sat down in the kitchen, went through the building order Mum had been given, and made notes.

Zoran kindly dropped around at eleven o’clock with a small bunch of government flowers for Mum, as a gesture of support. Mum thanked Zoran for such beautiful daisies.

“What did you say the name is?” Zoran asked.

“Daisies,” Mum repeated.

Zoran shook his head. "Stupid name. I prefer *Bellis perennis.*"

Zoran told Mum he hoped that the good guys would win, though from his experience this never happened.

By the end of the day, Mum had rung eleven TV and radio stations, but not one was interested that the SLC had been closed down. Our local MP didn't return Mum's call. It was sad to think that Mum's pride and joy might actually be something people didn't care about. There were always letters in the local paper complaining that the government money given to the SLC should be spent on roads, and not getting the long-term unemployed off the dole. Maybe the Kinglet community would be happier if the SLC was closed down forever?

"Don't feel depressed, Zilla," said Dad that night, as we shared a shriveled roast chicken. "I have a brilliant plan."

"What is it, Eric?"

"I can't tell you yet because it's not entirely complete. But it is brilliant. Still not hungry, Seth?"

"No."

Jack found the wishbone. I broke it with him and this time I got the bigger half. I wished for world peace. I did not wish for Miranda to be in love with me. That was never going to happen. Why waste a perfectly good wish?

The next day Dad sprang into action. He rang everybody who'd been in his carpentry class, starting with Damon.

Dad told Damon that he needed his assistance. Damon thought Dad said "sisters" and replied that he didn't have any. Dad explained very loudly that Damon was needed for a working bee. It would commence at the SLC first thing in the morning. "Wear protective clothing," Dad said. "Tell all your friends." Damon yelled that he would.

Then Dad went to our school's woodwork department and asked if he could borrow tools for tomorrow. The woodwork teacher, Mr. Sarkesian, refused because all his students were supposed to be making spice racks. Dad asked Mr. Sarkesian if the world really needed more spice racks. Mr. Sarkesian had a brief personal crisis. He said he'd never liked spice racks but they were on the syllabus. He also said he'd like to be part of the working bee. He'd bring his students. They hated spice racks, too.

By the end of the day the word was out. Something big was going to happen at the SLC. Even though the Center was closed, Zoran refused to desert the flowerbeds. He was putting down snail pellets when I saw him. (I'd been sent on a mission to buy more wheatgrass for Mum. She'd gone through half a paddock in the last two days.)

"What you doing, Set?" asked Zoran.

"My mum needs wheatgrass."

"This is grass you buy in health-food shop?"

I nodded.

"Health-food shop run by criminals," said Zoran. "Charge five dollars for seaweed. Pass me widger, please."

"What's a widger?"

Zoran rolled his eyes and picked up a shiny steel gardening implement from his barrow.

"This is widger. You need learn English."

"I'd better go before the shop closes," I said.

"What is wrong, Set? You have face like smacked bum."

"Everything is wrong."

Zoran shrugged. "Center is closed. Could be worse. Could be destroyed by atom bomb. But Center still here. Center will open again."

"Do you really think so?"

"No. I say to cheer you up."

"Actually, it's not just the Center I'm worried about."

"Is it the Miranda girl?"

I nodded. "She doesn't love me."

Zoran got to work with his widger. "Don't talk cacka," he said.

"Zoran, it's not cacka."

"We see how Miranda look at you when we go to *Elephant Man*. She love you all right. Like snail love *Physostegia virginiana*."

"She might've liked me back then. She doesn't any more. I did something really stupid."

"We all do stupid things, Set. Is Australia. We is allowed to make mistakes. Miranda will come back."

"I don't think so."

"Neither do I. But Mrs. Zoran does. And she much smarter than Zoran."

•

That night Dad stopped sleeping on the couch and returned to the master bedroom.

The next day, Mum explained to our school principal that the war against petty bureaucracy looked like it might go on for a bit longer. Could Jack and I be excused from school again? The principal told Mum that'd be fine, provided the war against petty bureaucracy didn't last for longer than a week.

The first to arrive at the Shared Learning Center was Elizabeth Taylor, wearing overalls. The next six to arrive were all Elizabeth's girlfriends whom she'd talked into helping. Before long, thirty kids had gathered. Dad and Mr. Sarkesian divided the kids into smaller groups then distributed tools, bits of timber and hard hats. Dad opened the doors of the Center and everyone got to work.

Mum arrived at ten thirty. She'd been organizing a deal with Mr. Racina to get free timber and other materials. Mum had to promise Mr. Racina that she'd arrange to have his daughter Poppy's poetry published in a book. It seemed like a deal with the devil, but these were desperate times.

Dad smiled to see Mum looking like the battler of old, the one who'd lain in front of bulldozers, the champion of the brown boobies.

Jack and India arrived at eleven. They'd been busy charging up their psychokinetic powers. They sat on a knoll, joined hands and looked at the Center. Their expressions were intense. I didn't see a single tool or piece of wood move on its own.

I barely thought of Miranda at all and the smell of Dencorub did nothing for me. The only reason I'd tucked the tube into my overalls was that I thought someone at the working bee might need it.

Under the lino in one of the learning rooms, Mum and I found some old brown pages from the local newspaper. There was a picture of the Phantom Pig from ten years ago. There was also a big story about the famous bushfire that had blazed through the shire and up the mountain. I was old enough to remember it. Jack and I were sent to Gran's place while Dad and Mum stayed behind to help fight the blaze. The headline on the paper was BUSHFIRE HORROR—POLICE SUSPECT ARSO.

More and more people, young and old, came to help. Casper and Jasper appeared and started chasing each other with chisels. Mr. Sarkesian took away their tools and gave them a special job—taking drinks to the workers. The twins took their responsibility seriously and ran around with water bottles.

The photographer from the local paper arrived and got the kids to pose for a nice group photograph. He told them to point at the SLC. The paper's reporter asked Dad for an interview. Dad told him we were all working together to correct the mistakes of the past. It sounded like rule seventeen from the Mr. Right list. When the reporter asked for Dad's name, he said it was Dr. William Shatner.

I helped Dad load some of the rotten old floorboards onto Mr. Sarkesian's ute.

"I found something rather intriguing in my toothbrush mug," said Dad.

"Was it a toothbrush?"

"That wouldn't be an intriguing thing to find."

"I guess not."

"It was a list somebody had torn out of *Dolly* magazine. Do you know anything about it?"

"Nothing," I said.

"I wonder who put it there?"

"An idiot," I said.

"I don't think the list is idiotic."

"It doesn't work. I thought it did once, but it doesn't."

"And you don't know who put it there?"

"Some fool."

"Well, I'd like to thank this fool. You see, the list worked for me. I'd like to give this fool some sort of reward."

"Is it money?"

"I'm not very rich at the moment. But it's quite a good reward. Perhaps I could just leave it for him somewhere? Where would a fool be likely to find a reward, do you think?"

"How big is it?"

"Quite small. About the size of a kumquat."

"In the cupboard under the sink in the kitchenette," I said. "If you leave something in the cup with a cat on it,

I'm sure the fool will find it."

Dad brushed some cobwebs out of my hair, then leaped back when he realized there was a spider there as well. I shook my head and the spider flew off and landed on Casper, who made it his pet. Elizabeth Taylor walked by, carrying a plastic bin full of plaster sheeting off-cuts. She winked at me, as if carrying a plastic bin full of plaster sheeting off-cuts was a pretty sexy thing to be doing.

"I really wouldn't bother about that list, Dad," I said. "It's not that great."

"Don't forget rule twenty-one, Seth. There's always rule twenty-one."

Not far away, Damon screamed at the top of his lungs when he discovered human remains under the rotten floorboards. They turned out to be two dead possums.

More and more people came to help. Doors were reattached so that they opened outward and not inward, moldy hessian was ripped down, wonky floorboards were replaced and the kitchenette was scoured so that it shone as never before.

At dusk we received a visit from the environmental health officer for the district of Currawong.

"We've fixed everything on your list," Dad told Mr. Raven, in front of the exhausted crowd. "Will you please reopen the Center?"

"The Center cannot be used if it's a danger to public health," said Mr. Raven. "Our building department will have to inspect it thoroughly."

"When will they be able to do that, do you think?"

"It's not for me to say. They are very busy people. I myself won't be able to inspect the kitchenette until April at the earliest, so I can't see the Center reopening before then."

There was a groan of disappointment from the crowd.

"I'm sorry!" said Dad.

"I must go," said Mr. Raven.

"I'm very sorry for flicking poo at you!" said Dad.

Mr. Raven turned. "I beg your pardon?"

Dad held his head high and spoke to Mr. Raven in a loud and convincing way. "I'm very sorry for *deliberately* flicking manure at you, Mr. Raven. It was highly disrespectful. You were just doing your job. And it was even more disrespectful of me to pretend it was an accident."

"Any fool could see it wasn't," Mr. Raven said.

"Which is why I'm apologizing to you sincerely, in front of all these people, from the bottom of my heart," declared Dad. "A lot of people have been put out, Mr. Raven, and it's my fault, because I flicked a piece of manure at you in anger and didn't apologize immediately, as I should have. I'm also sorry for calling you chromedome, which was a stupid and childish insult. Please accept my deepest, humblest apologies."

People clapped but Mr. Raven seemed unmoved.

I stepped forward. "And *I* am sorry, Mr. Raven. I'm sorry for calling you a pain in the arse."

The onlookers murmured and exchanged looks.

"Most of all," I continued, "I'm sorry for using your credit card to have six Portaloos delivered to your house. It was a terrible, idiotic thing to do. I'm sorry for the mental anguish caused to you and your wonderful daughter and your cat."

Mr. Raven was surprised. This was obviously the first he'd heard of my dreadful deed. Miranda hadn't told him after all.

Dad looked at me in amazement. "Seth?"

"It was me, Dad. I wish I'd told you before. But I just didn't get around to it. If we both go to jail we can ask for a twin cell."

"And *I* am sorry, Mr. Raven," yelled Damon. "I'm sorry for throwing a balloon full of water at you, even though I missed."

"And *I* am sorry, Mr. Raven," said Elizabeth Taylor. "I'm sorry for making that rude sign about Currawong Council. What I did was wrong. I'm also sorry for spray-painting POOFS LIVE HERE on the fence of a house in Kinglet, even though this doesn't affect you directly. It was bad of me to be mean to poofs because they're human beings like the rest of us."

There were startled looks from the crowd and more applause. The bellbirds excitedly went *ping!* They knew something special was going on.

Zoran stepped forward. "I am sorry for nothing at all," he told the crowd.

When it was clear that there were no more sorries, the senior environmental health officer for the district of

Currawong spoke to Dad. He wasn't interested in anyone else. "Society has its rules, Mr. Parrot. They are there for a reason and I respect them, even if there are those who do not. The Center will remain closed until a comprehensive investigation ..."

"Dad, they apologized!"

Miranda emerged from the crowd, looking as determined and unstoppable as Sigourney Weaver wearing that big yellow robot thing in *Aliens*.

"Miranda, go home," yelled Mr. Raven.

"Back off, Dad," Miranda yelled back. Then she lowered her voice and spoke gently. "Back off, or you'll lose me, too."

Miranda walked over to me and held my hand. I couldn't believe it. Our calluses rubbed and my head spun. Dad looked at Miranda, then at Mr. Raven, then at me. My secret was out. Dad looked astonished. Then he burst out laughing.

"What are you doing here?" I asked Miranda.

"That was a very sweet message, Carrot."

"What message?"

"The one you left on the answering machine."

"I didn't think your machine was working."

"It's not. Someone else got the message and gave it to me."

"When?"

"Just a little while ago."

"Who?"

"I'm sworn to secrecy."

Miranda squeezed my hand. This was seriously romantic behavior.

"Miranda, can I ask you a question?"

"Yes, Carrot."

"Do you know where kilts come from?"

"Scotland?"

"No, France. Isn't that interesting?"

"Not really, Carrot."

"That isn't actually what I wanted to ask."

"I'm glad."

I took a deep breath. "Miranda, do you think there's the slightest possibility that at some stage in the not-too-distant future you might become my serious girlfriend?"

"Yes, Carrot."

"I'm really, truly sorry about the Portaloos."

"You should be."

"Do you think your dad'll press charges?"

Miranda shook her head. "I doubt it. He's the one who blew up your letterbox."

My hand was now quite sweaty but Miranda continued to hold it.

FACT SEVENTEEN

An ostrich's eye is bigger than its brain

Miranda and I sat on a log and gazed at the river for a few moments. We pashed madly, then we gazed at the river again. Beautiful dragonflies hovered delicately over the sunlight-dappled water, and the bellbirds ate them, proving how disgusting nature can be.

"My gran's right," I said. "I can see into your soul."

"What do you see?"

"Wonderful things. All the colors of the rainbow. Roman rings. Camping equipment."

"Why are you so weird, Carrot?"

"I can't help it. It's the way I was brought up."

As the bellbirds enjoyed their feast, the carp in the river ate dirt, proving there are more revolting things to eat than dragonflies.

"I saw a statue of Venus," said Miranda. "That beautiful lady you mentioned. She didn't have arms. And she had really bad hair."

"You have good hair and arms," I said.

"So do you, Carrot. When are you going to ask me around? I want to see what your home is like."

"It's just a home," I shrugged. "It isn't anything to write

home about. There'd be no point, since whoever you were writing to would already be very familiar with what you were writing about."

"I'd still like to see it, Carrot."

"There's plenty of time."

We watched more dragonflies being eaten, and sighed. We were serious girlfriend and boyfriend.

"How did you find out it was your dad who blew up our letterbox?" I asked.

"He didn't actually do it himself. Fire freaks him out. There were some kids outside our house and they kept chanting 'chromedome chromedome chromedome' every night. In the end Dad went mad. He paid them to go away and set off crackers in your letterbox. I don't think he intended them to use so many."

"He told you all that?"

"No, the kids rang him and tried to blackmail him. I listened on the other line."

"So that's why he confiscated the fireworks at the Earthlight Festival."

"No, Carrot. He did that because he's a very good environmental health officer. I don't think he worked out the plan to blow up your letterbox until after he had the fireworks and got worked up. It wasn't exactly an ingenious plan."

"He could have blown up a kid!"

"They were very annoying kids."

"True."

"My dad went off the deep end for a while," said Miranda.

"So did mine."

"But he's getting better."

"Does he mind me seeing you?"

"He'll just have to get used to it."

Ping!

"Let's have a swim," Miranda said.

"My underpants aren't suitable," I said.

"You don't have to wear your underpants. And I don't have to wear my underpants either. There's no one here."

Was Miranda serious? I could hardly breathe for excitement. Chairman Mao Chairman Mao Chairman Mao. As I started unbuttoning my shirt, I noticed there were two nude Serbians in the water. They had come out of nowhere.

"Hello, Zoran," I called sadly.

"I am not Zoran," the Serbian man replied. "Zoran would never swim naked."

"Don't be idiot, Zoran," said Mrs. Zoran.

"Now you have given us both away, crazy woman! If we was in Serbia we would be fed to bears."

"Shut up, Zoozoo!" Mrs. Zoran splashed her husband.

For the first time ever, I heard Zoran laugh.

"We can still swim," Miranda said to me.

"No, it's okay. I'm not a racist, but I don't think I could swim with naked Serbians."

"Set," cried Mrs. Zoran. "You smart boy to like Oscar Wilde."

And I knew whose answering machine I'd reached that night when I'd poured out my heart.

•

Miranda and I rode our bikes toward Gang Gang. On the way, we were headed off by George Jupitus. The giant thug leaped off his bike and threatened to smash my stupid ugly face in. I crouched down.

"Come any closer," I said, "and I'll jumpkick you in the head."

I'd never do it, of course. Not after what happened to Jack. But George didn't know that.

"Get lost, George!" said Miranda.

The ex-boyfriend shook his head in puzzlement. "Why are you hanging around with this freak?"

"He's ... interesting," said Miranda.

Usually when you say that about someone, it's bad. You call someone "interesting" if you don't fancy them. But it sounded special the way Miranda said it. It made me think we'd be together for quite a few summers.

"Miranda, this guy is a total dweeb," George spat. "He's no good for you."

Miranda crouched down alongside me. Her leg muscles were taut, ready to unleash their awesome power. One leap and George would end up in the river. "I told you to get lost!" said Miranda.

George kicked some dirt with his heel, then backed off. "Psychos!" He mounted his bike. "You're both psychos. You deserve each other."

George Jupitus rode away. My serious girlfriend and I continued along the track.

•

That night I decided to rewrite my play as a comedy. I turned the terrifying Angel of Death into a bureaucrat. I gave him a dopey personal assistant who kept getting the paperwork wrong. I made the parents bicker all the time so that Death could hardly get a word in. I made the two kids into little terrors who kept pinching each other and tormenting Death by flicking elastic bands at him. I changed the next-door neighbor into a likeable clown character who makes Death feel guilty and want to join a circus. And finally, I had the grandmother challenge Death to a contest. I'd seen a film where Death plays chess, but I thought it'd be funnier if the contest was an arm wrestle. I changed the ending so that the grandmother wins the arm wrestle (she has amazing upper-body strength for a pensioner) and sends Death on his way. And I decided to rename my play *I'm Being Stalked by a Moonshadow*, because it sounded funnier.

I'm Being Stalked by a Moonshadow probably wasn't such a great play, though everyone was kind about it. The actors were all good, especially Tyrone and Poppy. But the best of all was quiet Lukas, who was very funny as Death's dopey personal assistant. He kept jumping back in alarm when perfectly ordinary things happened. He'd obviously been watching Karen use the photocopier. Casper and Jasper were good stage managers. They were far too busy to bite each other.

The local paper had this to say:

> I'M BEING STALKED BY A MOONSHADOW is a darkly comic play that Kinglet residents

will be talking about for many days to come. It's writer, local 14-year-old writer Seth Partot, clearly has a bright future ahead of him. The story involves a typical family receiving a visit from a mysterious stranger who turns out to be the Angel of Death, although people should not see the play knowing this as it spoils a clever twist in the plot. Local 13-year-old actors Jack Patrot and India German aquit themselves well in the role of the mother and father. Local baker Tyrone Schilling (21) is excellent in the title role and clearly has a bright future ahead of him. Though one must also single out talented local performers Poopy Racina, Nangret Braine and Lukas Hardwick for particular praise in their respective roles. All are 13, except for Lukas who is 9 and Nangret who is 12. According to program notes provided by director William Stretton, the play is a comedic representation of the confusing and ultimately alienating world in which we live today and this reviewer agrees holeheartedly. Mr. Stretton is 137 and clearly has a bright future ahead of him. Almost everything about this production works and it is a thoroughly satisfying night of world-class theater. The next production at the SLC will be *Romeo and Juliet* by William Shakespeare (dead).

Miranda told me she liked my play, but it would have

been better if Death hadn't been so fat. The closing-night party was at Tyrone's house, so of course it was brilliant. Thank God Jack and India were over their nudism phase. I invited Miranda to the party. But she wanted to stay home with her father. It was the anniversary of the terrible time that her mother, Ariel, died in the bushfire ten summers ago. Miranda spent the evening quietly with her dad, looking through all the scrapbooks that contained hundreds of pictures of her mother. I guess I'd be pretty hard to get along with if something like that happened to Miranda.

I'm still going around with Miranda. Her father no longer hates me. Now it's just strong dislike. I'm working on him, using a few tricks I've picked up from the Mr. Right list. When Miranda and I kickbox together we're in heaven. She may not have the best imagination in the world, but I have too much, so we balance each other as perfectly as the yin and the yang on Dad's necklace. Miranda doesn't like it when I wear it. But since it's Dad's favorite, and since he left it in the cat cup for me, I wear it a lot.

In my own universe, I've christened earth's moon Yin/Yang.

FACT EIGHTEEN

In the French town of Trie-Sur-Baise there is an annual festival where people impersonate pigs

Zoran ended up getting a job as an accountant, but he does voluntary work at the SLC garden every weekend.

Franca and Vincenzo continue to break up and get back together again. At the moment the salon is called Franca's Hair and Legs and Nails and Solarium.

The cost of hire and transportation of six Portaloos for a day was fifteen hundred dollars. Someone had to pay the company, and of course that someone was me. I worked for months delivering our local paper to get the money.

Jack broke up with India in the winter of 2000, and since then he's had three hundred girlfriends. He believes he is suffering from a condition called satyriasis, which is a psychological disorder that makes you think about sex all the time. It affects mainly teenage boys. Since then, Jack has suffered from hundreds of interesting conditions such as narcolepsy (falling asleep), insomnia (not falling asleep), polythelia (having an extra nipple), syndactyly (having webbed toes) and anseriphobia (fear of geese).

Dad started organizing trivia nights at the Center. The real champion was Lukas. Everyone wanted him on their team. So, always remember to keep an eye on the quiet ones, because they often know more than they let on.

Mum pulled an amazing stunt on Jack one night. She poked out her tongue at him and there was a little gold stud right in the middle of it. It was a magnetic one that she'd bought from Mr. Ha the chemist. Jack freaked out. Mum and Dad laughed so hard, the bellbirds fell out of the trees. It was great to hear them laugh together again.

We finally did get to Kruger National Park in 2001, but Jack wasn't allowed on safari because he refused to stop wearing his duty-free skin products and the smell freaked out the animals. He was happy to stay back at the lodge, swimming in his Lycra and chatting up girls.

One of the great mysteries of life was solved that summer. Dad said that when he'd gone next door to Mr. Robbins's house to return the car keys, he'd glimpsed a mysterious bundle in the hallway. It was a dry-cleaning bag. Dad swore it contained a pig costume.

We never found out who reported us to Mr. Raven on the day of the rendering. But we're certain it wasn't the Phantom Pig.

ERRATUM

Penguins don't actually like bananas.

APPENDIX I

Peace

By Poppy Racina (11)

People really should not fight,
Hurting others isn't right,
See how violent people are!
Watch that man explode a car!
Someone's burning down those huts!
Honestly, it drives me nuts!
Violent actions make me mad!
Violent words are just as bad!
But it's better to ignore
Insults that can lead to war,
I would rather live in peace
With my dog, who's called Denise.

APPENDIX II

22 Ways to Know If He Is Mr. Right

1 He takes an interest in your hobbies and pastimes.
2 He gives thoughtful and inventive presents.
3 He takes pride in his appearance.
4 He keeps his promises.
5 When he says, "I'm sorry," he looks you in the eye.
6 He is honest.
7 He is a good listener.
8 He never laughs at your dreams.
9 He does not declare war.
10 He never judges you by your relatives.
11 He is communicative.
12 He flosses.
13 He does not believe all he hears.
14 He says "Bless you!" when you sneeze.
15 He is not vain.
16 He remembers the three R's:
Respect for others.
Respect for himself.
Responsibility for all his actions.
17 When he realizes he has made a mistake he tries to fix things.
18 He is patient.
19 He understands when you need to be alone.
20 He knows how to keep your secrets.
21 He never gives up without a fight.
22 He thinks *Dolly* is a very good magazine.